SAN SALVADOR

OR

AN ECHTRA NUA

by

R.N. CLARKE

ATHAS ET VERITAS

2023

SAN SALVADOR

OR

AN ECHTRA NUA

by R.N. Clarke

First published in 2023

Cloud Publishing, 117 Lisburn Road, Belfast, BT9 7AF

FOR FAMILY

FOR FRIENDS

FROM RORY

…mountains of clouds,

…skies of seas,

…isles of stars,

…rains of rocks

VOLUME ONE

I
Geronimo

II
Inferno

III
Bokoro

PREMIÈRE PARTIE

I
Geronimo

Roberto was falling.

When he started, he did not know.

Perhaps it was today, perhaps yesterday.

Where he was going did not matter.

Where he had come from mattered even less.

As he fell, for what was surely a long time already, he saw many others who had suffered his same fate. Some looked like they had been falling forever, others were still as neatly dressed as when they had left their workplaces. The heavier people appeared to be falling much quicker than he was, but, as he passed, he noticed that he recognised their faces, meaning they must have been the same characters he had met earlier.

Here was the drunken colonel smoking a cigar, and there, the fat lady re-reading the same page of her newspaper. They were surrounded by many others, but Roberto struggled to understand exactly who they were. Since he had been falling for such a long time, the sensation which makes us queasy had already passed. Roberto now felt more uncomfortable to think that at some point his journey would end. On and on he was falling, past swirling smoke and locked doors. He tried to remember the moment he had started to fall, but he had no memory of it. Closing his eyes, he started to wonder if perhaps he was moving upwards, and it was really the others around him who were falling. At that moment however, he was rudely awoken by the arm of the colonel landing on his shoulder. He opened his eyes and looked at the bearded face beside him.

'I see you're wondering what you're doing here, my young friend.'

'What was I doing before I got here?' replied Roberto.

'Dying,' the colonel added with a sigh.

At these words, the figure disappeared. Roberto continued to fall, further and further through this space between spaces, until at last he passed a fisherman. He adjusted his speed accordingly – for by now he had greatly adapted himself to this new way of being – and slowed down to the crawl at which the fisherman moved. Slightly surprised, but pleasantly calm, the old man admired how gracefully Roberto had reduced his speed, approving with a nod of his head.

'Were you also born of the sea?' he asked from below his moustaches.

'Well, I lived by it.'

'That's good enough,' the man said.

At this point, Roberto had mostly returned to what was once his normal speed. He still sensed that somewhere, out there in the darkness, there were objects falling, there were people moving, and life was happening, yet for as far as he could see around him, all stood still, all except for a warm breeze blowing in from the sea where the old fisherman had cast his line.

'Where are we?' Roberto asked.

'We're by the sea, dummy!' he responded.

'No, but *where* is that sea?' Roberto rebuffed him.

'Well, it's right there! Can't you see it?'

The man then gave Roberto an inquisitive look over the top of his round glasses.

'Haven't you ever been to the sea before?'

'Yes, I mean, I've been near it...'

'But not to this one, I bet. Even if you were to go and find a thousand oceans to swim across, you'd never find a sea quite like this one.'

Roberto stepped forward. There was a blinding flash of light – and suddenly he could smell the salty air of the sea. He could feel the thick wind as it pushed back his hair, and he saw that he had stepped out from a dark cave, onto a rocky beach, scattered with white sands which stretched for miles off into the distance.

'But where did I come from?' Roberto said quietly, looking back into the dark void behind him.

'Does it matter?' came the reply.

Roberto jumped at these words, having nearly forgotten the stony-faced chap who was still standing there beside him.

'All that matters is where you are going.' He made a good point. Roberto looked up at him, and saw a change had come over the fisherman. After this step into life, the fellow was now well-groomed, with a thick, curly string of hair below his long, hooked nose. He seemed younger, as if colour had been thrown into his life once more.

'Well, where we are now? What is this place called?' Roberto asked him.

'Different people call this place different things, since they all think different thoughts when they see it,' the mariner replied. 'Back when I was just about your age, I visited this place with a group of Spaniards, who called it San Salvador — the story goes that their forefathers had sailed for months & months on a grand old galleon but had not found any land whatsoever since their departure – until they got here, that is. I always liked that name myself, but over the years I've heard it called all sorts of things, most of which I couldn't bring myself to repeat.'

'Then San Salvador is what I will also call it,' Roberto replied triumphantly.

'Hmmm yes, very good,' the man chuckled, 'But who exactly are you going to talk to about it?'

Roberto looked around. The shoreline stretched out for miles in both directions, but not one sign of life could he find there. He looked inland, where, beyond the dunes and hills, there lay a virgin forest, where he could hear birds calling.

'Well, I can talk to you at least,' he said, looking back towards the fisherman, but he was gone. His equipment remained there, bobbing up and down in the gentle waves, though he himself had vanished. Before Roberto could call for him however, he noticed a tugging at the line. Not wanting to let the opportunity go to waste, Roberto took the rod and pulled with all his strength. The end of the line emerged from the water, and he pulled his catch towards the shore. On the hook was a bright green egg, around the size of an ostrich egg — however big that may be — and covered in some kind of seaweed. Roberto took it out from the tangle of kelp, and held it to his chest. Stepping back, he tried to call for the fisherman, but there was no response. The wind was growing progressively stronger since the moment Roberto had arrived on the beach, and it was now at the point of a gale. Seeing the forest close by, he ran to the shade of its wide branches, holding the egg under his jumper. The small dunes between the forest and the sea broke up most of the wind - so much so in fact, that it was rather pleasant there, beneath the thick leaves of the trees.

Roberto stopped to investigate the egg more closely, turning it slowly in his hands. He had only ever seen eggs at the breakfast table, and then he had at least a knife with which to break it - now he didn't even have a teaspoon.

'Whatever shall I do with it?' he wondered, 'If I smash it on the ground, it won't be fit for eating, if I keep it, hoping to find a restaurant, they might not even know what to do with it.'

'DON'T EVEN THINK ABOUT IT!' cried a shrill voice from the treetops. A shadow rustled and swooped down to a branch above Roberto's head.

'One more thought like that and I shall have to report you to the sheriff!' said the large bird.

'But I *have* already thought about it,' Roberto said to the well-dressed creature that stood above him.

'Well stop it this instant!' it replied, 'and I'll have you know that I am not an *'it'* — I am an owl — an owl with a name. My name is Alfred, and I am at your service, my good sir.' Alfred adjusted his suit-like feathers before turning his eyes back to the boy.

'I see you have one very special object in your hands there,' glancing sharply at the egg. 'This is no ordinary bird egg that you have in your possession, wherever could you have found such a thing?'

'Il... uh...c'est venu de la mer,' Roberto replied in a language he had heard once in his childhood, on his summer holidays abroad.

'Excuse me?!' the bird interrupted indignantly 'AND I'm not just any old bird! I have a name, please use it! But please, continue, you pulled it from the ocean, correct?'

Roberto continued in French, thinking it polite, but also knowing that all birds can understand you, if you just learn to speak how *they* speak. Alfred listened closely, but after Roberto had finished speaking, Alfred confessed that he was actually a German owl, and had only understood some of his story.

'Anyway, it doesn't matter where this egg came from, what matters is what it will grow into,' he added.

Roberto looked down at the egg and noticed that it had started to show hints of a lighter shade of brown. Alfred moved closer to investigate it, saying, 'Hmm yes, this is a very important egg, why, I do believe it is the egg of an island spirit, but you mustn't let *it* know that.'

Roberto had heard of spirits in books before, but had always assumed they were something you couldn't touch, like a heart.

'You *can* touch a person's heart; you just have to do something nice for them,' Alfred said, looking down his glasses at Roberto.

'How did you know what I was thinking about?' Roberto exclaimed, shocked by this intrusion into his thoughts.

'Well you shouldn't think about these things so loudly then, if you don't want people listening in!' came the response. The boy ran his hand over the smooth, almost wooden, surface of the oval that he held. A slight glow sparkled around it, and he felt his hand warmed where he touched it.

'Yes, it seems it likes the forest, you should take it further inside.'

'But it came from the ocean, would it not be better to take it back?'

'My dear boy, it doesn't matter where it came from, what matters is where it's going! Hasn't anyone ever told you that? Besides, you said it was lying in a bed of seaweed, no? Then it must have come from one of those underwater forests, and EVERYONE knows that all those dirty green things that wash up on the beach are just trees trying to find their way back to the forest.'

Roberto wasn't sure if this was true or not, but since Alfred said it with such care and confidence, it must have been correct.

'You change the topic quite a lot, don't you?' Roberto replied.

'Why yes, of course, I like to do so, since I find change to be quite becoming for a young man. In fact, a great philosopher once said, 'Changes in

11

the world around us are not accidental, rather, they form part of the essence
of the univer—'

'Yes, ok, I get it, you've told me a lot, but nothing about this island,
or why I'm here, or even what a spirit is!' Roberto interrupted.

As he said this however, he felt a gust of wind push him from
behind, which blew straight through the leaves and straight through Alfred!
The distinguished fellow disappeared into thin air, and a small stone fell from
the branch that he once stood upon. Roberto rushed forward to pick it up,
slipping it into his pocket as he ran further into the forest.

Once he was safe from the strong breezes beyond the trees, he
stopped to admire the wooden paradise he now found himself in. There were
birds tweeting above him, and bugs chirping cheerfully in the undergrowth
below. It seemed like everywhere he looked, there was life blossoming,
crimson butterflies danced over his head, and long blue dragonflies darted
quickly past him. Looking down at the egg, he noticed it was developing a
deep nutty acorn colour, somewhere between green and brown.

Roberto saw a small path leading further into the woods. He went
forward, taking care not to disturb nature's thousand waltzes taking place
both above and beneath him. The egg was heavy, and after some time he
came across a clearing with a stump at its centre. He sat down on it to
examine the strange object, and noticed three dark green dots had appeared
on the middle of it.

'It must be ready to hatch!' he thought, and jumped up from his seat,
hoping to find a bird who could help (for, as you surely know, birds know an
awful lot about eggs) but there was silence in all directions. Suddenly a gust,
much like the one before, and still wet with the salt from the sea, knocked the
egg from Roberto's arms! It bumped the stump and landed in a pile of leaves
nearby. The boy ran to check on it, but to his surprise, when he turned it, he

12

saw two bright eyes looking back at him. A pair of ears popped out from its sides, and a button nose sat above a long, frowning mouth.

'THANKS for the wake-up call, I was quite cosy in there you know!' the egg grumbled.

'I'm so sorry! It was the wind!' Roberto hastily responded.

'Ah it's always the wind, isn't it? Anyway, whatever it was, I'm awake now, so let's go,' it said with a look of determination in its eyes.

'But where to?' Roberto asked.

'To where we're going of course!' it said as it hopped blithely through the auburn leaves. Roberto watched as an acorn and a maple leaf were drawn towards the egg, orbiting around it like magnets, swirling below its mouth, as it then shifted its weight forward and tried to roll, before falling flat on its face.

'I'll be here for hours at this rate,' it sighed, spitting a bit of mud from its lips, 'If only you'd have let me sleep, I'd have been ripe by the time I fell!'

'I told you, I'm sorry, I didn't mean to drop you!' Roberto repeated.

'What do you mean you didn't mean to drop me? Of course you did! Why do you think seeds fall from trees? They can't stay up there forever you know! What's your name anyway?'

'Me? I'm Roberto. I don't know much more than that.'

'All you really need to know is yourself,' the egg grinned, 'I'm Geronimo, though I don't know much more than that either.'

'Well, you know where you're going, which is more than I knew when I was born — back then I didn't even know my own name!'

'You mean you didn't name yourself the first thing that popped into your head when you were born?' Geronimo said, the shock obvious on his face.

13

'No, my parents named me Roberto when I was born. They even spent years teaching me their language — how do you know how to speak already?'

'Huh, I never thought about it really. I guess I just listened more, back when I was older.'

'I think you mean younger, no?' Roberto interjected.

'No, I think I mean older,' said the little ball as it rolled forward again, and collapsed in the leaves.

'Let me give you a hand there,' Roberto said, moving towards Geronimo.

'No thank you!' came the poor grumble from Geronimo, his mouth still stuck to the ground, 'I have to get there on my own bat,' spitting out some leaves as he rolled back. Roberto felt obliged to help somehow, watching the poor thing roll about.

'Where are you going?' Roberto asked.

'Where are WE going, I think you mean! Unless you've got other plans, in which case it's fine. I'll be going to the mountain, feel free to join me,' and Geronimo set off, clumsily rolling in that painfully awkward side-to-side motion in which eggs tend to move. Roberto followed the now-living creature as it moved forward with determination, stumbling and hitting its face on the ground as it went. The ground was filled with orange leaves and fallen seeds, which made Roberto think it was now Autumn, even though mere minutes before, in the clearing, he was sure it seemed like the middle of Spring.

'What a mysterious place this is…' he thought to himself.

'A mysterious place indeed,' said a voice from above. They jumped at this unexpected comment, especially Geronimo, for Roberto knew at once that this was the voice of Alfred.

'But I just watched you disappear in that gust of wind!' Roberto cried out in joy and surprise in equal measure, 'How did you get here?'

'The things we love are like the leaves of the tree, they could fall at any moment with a gust of wind.' replied Alfred with a knowing smile.

'Do you two know each other? How on earth did a boy and a bird become friends?' Geronimo piped in.

'People with much less in common than us can become friends,' Alfred said slowly, examining the egg inquisitively, 'You just have to—'

'Well, what's your name?' Geronimo interrupted, before the bird could continue his lecture.

'Why, I do believe I have already introduced myself to you, though I suppose you *were* so much older then, and perhaps you have forgotten. My name is Alfred, and I—' '—am at your service my good sir.' Geronimo finished the sentence in unison with Alfred.

'You're right, you did introduce yourself to me — only, I can't for the life of me remember when.'

'Ah but you were much older then, when we last met. Anyway, you've called yourself Geronimo, correct?'

'Boy you sure do know a lot, don't you? Yes, I'm Geronimo,' he said with a proud hop, before bumping the ground again.

'You're smaller than I thought you'd be,' Alfred chuckled softly, 'but no matter, I'm sure you're destined for great things.' Geronimo wasn't sure if he was offended or not, but eventually decided the second half of the sentence rendered the statement more positive than negative.

'Alfred, do you know where we're supposed to be going?'

'Of course I do! In fact, I was just there, earlier tonight,' he obliquely responded.

'Can't you help us out by flying us there?'

'I could, but then how will you appreciate it when you get there? If everyone's story had a bird who just flew them here and there, no-one would ever build any character!' Alfred replied with a smirk.

'But why can you fly, and we can't? What makes you so special?'

'Oh, nothing makes me special, especially not wings, there are plenty of birds who have wings on their arms. Yet, I *have* earnt these wings, for all the hours I've spent going here and there by foot. Nevertheless, I will always be at your service, my good sir. Have you thought about walking uphill?' Alfred turned his head in that strange way that owls often do, before adding, 'Remember, it is not your misfortune that these events should be your fate, rather it is your *good* fortune that you hold the strength to bear it,' and with that, he flew off into the direction of the wind, and was gone, leaving Roberto & Geronimo alone again.

'What a strange fellow. Anyways, let's go.' Geronimo said to break the silence.

As they walked, Roberto noticed the small spiral of air that swirled below the egg. It picked up some leaves and seeds as they moved, spinning there like a mini-cyclone - and in moments when it was particularly strong, it helped Geronimo to move rather swiftly across the forest floor. Then, almost as soon as it started to pick up traction, it fell away, leaving no more than the force of a long sigh, and Geronimo would fall and knock his face once again. Roberto walked slightly behind him, since the small creature seemed to know his way through the wood, which was now bathed in the soft gleam of early twilight. While the evening grew, and the stars came out from their dark hiding places, Roberto grew worried about where they would sleep that night, once the darkness had conquered the day.

'I'm sure someone will take us in,' said Geronimo, seemingly unaware, that the only other living being they had encountered that day was an owl who tended to disappear precisely whenever he was needed. Sure enough though, just as the final embers of the sun's rays slipped from the long green arms of the trees above, the two travellers spotted a small cabin up ahead, nestled between the edge of the forest and the banks of a gentle river.

Dimly lit by the chestnut glow of a small campfire burning beside it, the shelter seemed to be made from wood, and wasn't much bigger than where Roberto's father kept his shovels and rakes. Above the campfire there were three large fish roasting, and their strong scent got caught in Roberto's nose. Drawing closer, he noticed the outline of a figure lying against the cabin, with a cap pulled down to cover their face.

Trying not to startle the person, Roberto let out a short cough to announce their arrival, but this only served to make the shadowy shape jump up with surprise and knock over the thermos that rested on his thigh. Looking up to see where the source of this disruption had come from, the silhouetted eyes met Roberto's own, and the dull face brightened as he stood up.

It was the fisherman, who must have dozed off while he was preparing his dinner, in spite of the coffee he had been drinking from his flask. While he was startled at first - being awoken from his slumber - the man appeared pleased to see Roberto again, and intrigued by the odd ball that was moving beside him.

'You're late for your supper!' the fisherman announced as he pulled cutlery and dishes from the pockets of his overcoat, placing them carefully on a short table that stood nearby, 'No matter, you're here now, and that's the most important thing. Well — sit down!'

The table was set, and the fisherman moved back towards the fire. Roberto & Geronimo sat around the neatly decorated surface, Roberto crossing his legs as he sat down on the ground, Geronimo propping himself up on a tuft of grass. The fisherman pulled the fish from the flames, gently prodding them with a knife to check that they were cooked through. He pulled the long harpoons from the stakes above the fire, and stuck them into the ground beside the table.

'*Aprovecho!*' he grinned. Roberto cut himself a slice from the oily side of the long fish. Its face looked at him from beyond the grave world where its dark eyes now lived. A slight hint of guilt overtook him for a moment, before the fisherman's glare led him to take another cut of rubbery meat. Geronimo, quite unable to eat such a monstrous display of flesh, was grateful with but a simple dish of water, which he lapped up gleefully.

'It's good for your muscles, this merluza!' the fisherman said cheerfully as he showed Roberto the correct way to eat it, separating the flesh from bone.

'He's right y'know!' added Geronimo, 'I don't have any muscles so it wouldn't do me much good anyway.'

And there they sat for a quiet moment together, enjoying long slices of warm merluza by the fading fire. The stars were clearer now, and the calm cool night air began to settle in. Finishing their last bites, they looked up from their silence, and stood up to get ready to sleep.

Doing this woke them up from their sleepy post-meal trance, and Roberto began clearing up the table. Bringing the dishes inside the cabin, he noticed the roof was curved, like the hull of a boat. Three small neatly made beds were built into the wall, and on the other side, there stood a well-kept kitchenette. Geronimo hopped inside too, commenting in passing on the efficient use of space, and the tasteful décor.

Roberto remained quiet, the fisherman inspired a certain tranquillity in him, where he felt his actions spoke louder than words. The fisherman would respond in return with a smile and a nod. He was not as neat as when he had last seen him, nor was he as unkempt as their first meeting. Instead, he seemed like a perfect blend of all his previous selves, rolled into one. Roberto could tell this man's journey had been a long one, a journey that had started before any books were written, or monuments built. Every being that had come before him had led to the creation of this one person, perfectly imperfect.

Roberto's quiet internal serenity was broken by a plate slipping from his hand as he put it on the drying rack. His heart skipped a beat, but the fisherman, nimble as ever, calmly plucked the dish from its descent.

He replaced it on the rack more nonchalantly than Roberto had ever seen a word like that before! Once all the dishes were dried and returned to their cupboards and pockets, this rag-tag bunch of adventurers settled down to sleep, the fisherman on the top bunk, Geronimo on the bottom, and Roberto tucked in the middle.

When Roberto closed his eyes, visions of all the strange people and places he had seen that day drifted through his mind, and he watched as this strange assortment of shapes and figures interacted with each other, gradually becoming distorted in the growing darkness, until he was so far away from them all that he could no longer make out what they were laughing about.

II
Inferno

Roberto awoke suddenly. His body felt like stone as he pulled himself from the soft mattress. Light was already streaming in from the small window, and someone, presumably the fisherman, was making noise outside. After taking a moment to reflect on all the strange new things he had seen the previous day, he stood and stretched, and noticed he was alone in the cabin.

Opening the door, he was blinded briefly by the early sunlight, before seeing the fisherman and Geronimo sitting side by side, facing the river. Hearing the door open, they turned to face him, and greeted him with a cheery wave.

'There's coffee in the pot,' the fisherman smiled.

Taking the small copper kettle from above the fire, Roberto at first offered a top-up to the fisherman, then an extra drop for Geronimo, (who confessed he had drunk far too much already) before taking a metal cup from the table and pouring some for himself. The thick, dark liquid warmed his throat as he drank it, though he found it rather bitter compared to the hot coca he usually drank at breakfast. Nevertheless, it left a pleasing taste on his tongue, and he gulped it down. The fisherman pulled a packet of chocolate biscuits from his sleeve and offered them to Roberto.

'Dip them in your coffee,' he smiled, offering him the last drop, which everyone knows is the sweetest part. After they had splashed their faces in the rivers' cool waters, they began to discuss their next steps.

'Well I'm staying right here!' the fisherman resolutely remarked. Roberto didn't understand this comment. Considering the man's home could be turned upside down and moved along the river to wherever the fisherman might ever want to go - why would he just stay in one place?

'We need to get to the mountain.' Geronimo chirped in.

'I don't know where I'm going.' Roberto glumly added.

'Don't be so silly!' said Geronimo 'You're coming with me!'

'But where to?'

'To the mountain!'

Geronimo seemed confused by his hesitation to travel with him.

'Why shouldn't I just stay right here with the fisherman?' Roberto stubbornly replied. 'I can just as easily stay here and catch fish and live a simple life.'

'Oh, come on, you've never even caught a fish! The one time you tried to catch one, you caught some seaweed, with me inside!' Geronimo laughed as he said this, but the fisherman stood gravely by, watching his line's float for a bite. He felt Roberto's inquisitive gaze on his conscience, and turned to him.

'Son, I've seen this world, I've lived, I've travelled, now it's your turn. Go with your friend. I'll be ok here on my own.'

Casting his glance back to the waters, Roberto asked him, 'But where is this mountain? What's its name? How do we get there?'

'It has had many names, in many languages. It sounds silly to say it, but it's really quite beautiful. That's the first thing you notice about it, when you see it. Your first thoughts will always speak the name to you, when your eyes finally fall upon it. Have you never dreamt of a far-off mountain in your childhood slumbering? In those moments before you slip away, there grows a beautiful, symmetrical giant of rock, standing tall before a still lake, surrounded by a gentle evergreen forest, and all you can think is – I want to go there? That's its name.'

Roberto looked at him in astonishment, thinking over all that had been said. He then realised that the fisherman had only really answered one of his questions, and even then, he had barely answered that.

'Ok, but what about where it is?' he asked again.

'Uphill of course! Yip, just keep travelling north of here, following the river's course, and you'll find it soon enough.'

'Which direction is north though?'

'Why it's upstream ya dummy! Any more questions, kid?'

'I already asked it, but I guess I'll try it again - how do we get there?'

The fisherman's face dropped. He picked it up and put it back on, before looking at Roberto with a slightly disappointed gaze.
'You should never ask someone 'How' to do something. That's the most important part of learning - working out the 'How' yourself. My old schoolmaster would say 'Give a man a fish, he'll eat for a day, show a man a fish, he'll think for life.' That certainly got me this far. You'll find your own way, I believe in you. Your legs may be short, but you'll go far,' he said as he patted Roberto's shoulder.

The boy looked off into the distance, across the running stream, following the trees and bushes sprouting along its flanks. 'It's a long way, to be sure, but take your time, and stop off at places along the way. The journey is always more important than where you are going. Always enjoy the company you're with, and never live life in a hurry. There are more days than joys to fill them - take enjoyment slowly. Listen, there's a small town up ahead, why don't you see who you meet there, and maybe they'll help you find this mountain you're searching for,' having said his piece, he turned back to face the river.

Roberto & Geronimo thanked him for his help and turned upstream. Geronimo, as ever, struggled to push himself uphill. 'It's *absurd* that life has made me, a ball, spend it going uphill. Why ever did I come from the sea, to find this mountain?'

'You did it because you felt called to do it,' Roberto replied.

His small, rounded companion was inspired by this insightfulness.

'I *do* definitely feel myself growing stronger as time goes by. Look how many leaves I've gathered!'

Sure enough, there was a neat little pile of coloured leaves gathered in the slight updraft that blew beneath this odd floating creature.

'But what are you going to use them for?' Roberto asked, wondering why his friend was so preoccupied with the bundle of dust beneath him.

'I'm going to use them to grow!' his little friend replied, 'And by the time we get to the mountain, I'll be big and strong!'

'That's another thing, why is it so important that we get to this mountain?' Roberto asked as they walked.

'Don't worry, you'll see why soon enough, and from what the fisherman said, it should only be a couple of days away now.'

'Hoo-hooo,' croaked a shrill bird from above.

'Was that bird laughing at me?' said Geronimo, looking up, but seeing nothing there.

The two walked on, admiring the perfumed flowers and foreign fruit trees which were growing by the river.

'It's springtime already here it seems!' said Geronimo as he made Roberto pluck a pink rose to add to his pile of leaves, now blossoming many shades of green.

'Hoo-hooo,' mocked the same low birdcall as Geronimo said this.

'There it is again!' Geronimo shouted to the empty trees.

The pair continued walking now for some time, all the while feeling they were being watched from above.

'It didn't sound like Alfred, and I'm sure he would have said a Hoo-llo at least,' said Roberto, breaking the silence, 'Actually, I'm surprised we haven't seen him in all this time, I wonder where he could be.'

'Well, if we haven't seen him in all this time, then we're probably headed in the right direction. He told us to go North, and obviously the river is going uphill, so we should just stick with it. Anyway, we've been walking for a while now, isn't it about lunchtime?'

'Hoo-hoo,' the same call came again, however, this time, the pair managed to turn their heads quickly towards the sky, and above them they saw a small cuckoo-bird pull back its head from a branch.

'Hey you!' Geronimo shouted. The bird meekly poked its head from behind the cover, looking at the two strangers from left to right, left to right, left to right, before swiftly moving its head away.

'Do you understand me?' Geronimo asked.

'Hoo-hoo,' came the reply, the bird jerking its head forward to look at the pair during each of these 'Hoos.' Geronimo looked towards Roberto in amazement.

'I wonder if he understands me too,' said Roberto, looking up at the bird.

'Hoooo,' it responded sadly. Roberto remembered how Alfred had told him he was actually a German owl, and he thought that this one might be too, so he asked:

'Sprechen Sie Deutsch?' in as clear and upright a tone as he could manage.

'Alzoooo,' said the bird in response, sticking itself out from the branch once again and looking at the boy for a moment. 'Wo hast du das gelernt?'

24

Geronimo looked on as they spoke this strange language that he couldn't understand. Roberto, who continued in German, responded to the bird's question, saying,

'I don't know where I have learnt this, but we met a German owl yesterday called Alfred, perhaps you know him?'

'Ach! Then you are the boy I've heard so much about!' the cuckoo replied, shifting slightly to get a closer look at Roberto. 'Mmm, ja, very good. Tchja, of course I know Alfred, he's my brother!' Roberto laughed slightly at this, finding it hard to believe that two brothers could look so different, provoking a piercing stare from the bird.

'But you look nothing like him!' Roberto exclaimed.

'People can have a lot in common even if they don't look similar, especially if they were raised together!' then the bird continued to tell Roberto & Geronimo about his life, how he was always the smallest bird in their tree, how the other birds would mock him since he looked so different from the rest, and finally that his name was Albert.

'Life has not alv-vays been kind to a cuckoo-owl such as I,' he said wistfully, 'but zat doesn't matter really, there's enough life to go around, as long as you know how to spend your time. Hoo-hoo!' looking off into the distance as he spoke.

Geronimo, who had not understood much of the conversation, was instead playing with the flowers growing at the foot of the tree, bopping along in time with the strict rhythm which Albert was tapping out with his pitter-pattering bird legs.

After some time spent in conversation, Albert jumped quickly and landed on the next tree, in order to avoid the sunlight which was moving swiftly towards his perch. Roberto & Geronimo could not help but follow, and moved forward with him, before Albert then jumped on again.

'Come on boys!' he cried, 'Vee haff got to make some time up!' before hopping on, further into the trees. They followed him as he picked up speed, without really questioning where they were going.

As they went, Roberto thought to himself, 'What do those phrases mean? To make up time? To pick up speed? I've only ever made up stories, or picked up ideas, how could those things that don't really exist be made, or picked?'

Roberto picked one of the plump, peach-like fruits from the tree where Albert was sat, drumming on the wood. The fruit was dark purple, turning red, and covered all over by small bumpy pimples. Roberto squeezed it softly, feeling it was perhaps not at its ripest, but nonetheless ready for eating.

'Ah, I see tze gruppelberries are in season,' said Albert, peering at the fleshy fruit Roberto was holding.

'But how could it have grown so quickly?' Roberto asked, 'It looked like autumn yesterday evening!'

'Ach, my dear boy,' Albert replied, sounding more like his brother now, 'Everything has its season, if yours isn't today, perhaps it vill be tomorrow.'

Roberto bit into the foreign fruit, which tasted like an apple and grape mixed, with some sharp raspberry sweetness on top. He swallowed his piece and offered a bit to Geronimo, who hopped, crunched, and fell back down into his pile of daisies and grass trimmings, which was now growing quite large and very colourful.

Albert also took a bite before Roberto finished it off. Enjoying the pleasant aftertaste it left in his mouth, Roberto picked another for himself, and one for each of his travelling companions. Geronimo added it to the collection of greenery below, to save for later, and Albert pecked quickly at his, finishing it rapidly. They walked on.

The sun was just passing its highest point, and there were few clouds in the sky. The river widened, and the fruit that weighed down the branches of the trees on the other side now seemed very far away. Roberto looked into the running waters which divided the forest. Small silverfish were shooting past, dark grey rocks lined the riverbed, but even in the middle, it never seemed to go deeper than Roberto's knees. He watched it for a while, trying to work out what exactly was strange about it.

'I've seen rivers with fish. I've seen rivers with rocks. I've seen rivers with depth before, but there's something different about this one,' he thought this to himself as he walked.

Then, all of a sudden, it hit him. The river was flowing backwards! Its waters seemed to have broken free from gravity's pull, and were moving uphill, flowing away from the sea where they had met the fisherman. Roberto stopped, amazed by what he saw, and asked his companions if they did not find it strange that a river should run away from the sea.

'If *I* were a river, I would also run away from the sea. Once a river reaches the sea, it's no longer a river - it becomes one with the sea, and it loses its individuality. Now, if I knew there was someplace that would do that to me, I would also go in precisely the opposite direction,' stated Albert in a very matter-of-fact manner.

'I suppose that makes sense,' said Roberto, even if it didn't really. He instead thought of how water wishes to join water, and how youth wishes to join youth. They continued along the river's path, which ran with them as they walked. The tip of a tall tower appeared up ahead.

'Just as my father would say – There's always life by rivers,' thought Roberto as he pointed towards what he first thought was a spire, but was really an empty flagpole.

'Ah, it's from another era, this ruin,' Albert remarked, looking sadly towards it, 'Once upon a time, Two Queens, Hélène & Belén, lived there, now there is just rubble and wild animals. Time has worn away its grandeur, the days of its glories have passed.'

As they got closer, Roberto saw its walls were crumbling, its trees overgrown, and its wooden gates, rotting.

'It was beautiful in its day,' Albert sighed.

'It still is!' cried Geronimo, 'Just because animals live there now, doesn't make it any less of a castle!'

There was indeed a certain beauty to those tumbled-down piles of mossy stone, pulsating with thousands of tiny creatures going to-and-fro, mice and squirrels, ants and ladybirds, spiders and geckoes, calmly going about their work in the early afternoon sun. Perhaps there was once a kingdom here, but now, there stood hundreds, each of them contributing to the formation of the eco-system in their own unique way. Legions of worker ants, families of squirrels, all living side-by-side within the confines of these castle walls. Even if a Queen was still to live here, her word would have no power over these groups of individuals, all in total and indivisible control of their own destinies.

Coming now before the castle's rundown entrance, it seemed to shine with its own decrepit splendour. Roberto could feel the weight of its history, the battles fought, and the lives lost there, as the façade bore down upon them.

'Let's go inside!' shouted Geronimo, causing a passing badger to jump with surprise. Roberto looked on towards its dark interior, wondering what might else might live within. Albert looked apprehensive at this idea, but eventually agreed to it, saying:

'I suppose it's just another part of the forest now, and nothing dangerous has lived in this place for a long time.'

Through the stone arch they passed, arriving in a small courtyard. Four fruit trees were growing, their branches weighed down by an abundance of unpicked black balls. They were unlike anything Roberto had seen before, and had small sharp points around their body. He picked one carefully, so as not to cut his fingers, but found that it took a lot of strength to remove the thick stem from the gnarled black wood. With some force however, he managed to break it loose, and the whole tree shivered backwards when it was set free, unripe and before its time.

A sharp pain shot from his hand, up his arm, and through the right side of his chest. Looking into his right palm, where he held the odd object, he saw its spikes had pierced the skin on his hand in many places. Blood trickled slowly down along his wrinkles, crimson streams taking their first steps towards becoming rivers. Geronimo and Albert looked on in shock, as small drops now began to drip on the ground below, while Roberto just stared at the red liquid, the very essence of his own life, coming forth to greet him.

'Take this!' Geronimo shouted, knocking the black ball to the ground, and offering up the gruppelberry he had kept from earlier. As Roberto moved to take the fruit from Geronimo's pile, the pain began to settle in. He felt lightheaded, and the very sensation of feeling had disappeared from his hand. Limply moving it toward Geronimo, breathing weakly, he touched the fruit, and a great wave of relief washed over him.

He regained his natural breathing pattern, his clouded mind was cleared, and his fingertips tingled. He rolled the fruit into the palm where once this other, foul object had caused him such fleeting, yet intense pain. The bleeding stopped and the fruit appeared to clean his hand as he moved it back and forth. Pins and needles began to rumble down his arm, through his wrist, then stretching out into his fingers. Squeezing the gruppelberry, he found it to be much softer than when he had held it before, and its colour had deepened into a thick scarlet - with a hint of bronze reflecting too when the light fell just right. The pain had, by now, mostly subsided, and he turned to face his friends.

'I should have known it was a bad fruit,' he said guiltily, looking down at the barbed orb which lay before him.

'There's no such thing as a bad fruit! Every fruit is tasty to some beast or another,' said Geronimo as he moved forward to inspect it. He poked its jagged exterior lightly, before looking up at Roberto.

'Don't you want to find out what's inside it?' Geronimo asked, but Roberto could hardly look at the fruit without remembering the pain that it had caused him.

'No, I've had enough of that…thing, and I don't care to see it again.'

Saddened by Roberto's downcast tone, Geronimo's face dropped. It must have been a real problem in that country, but he quickly picked it back up.

'What about…' said Geronimo, smiling slightly, 'We make a trade. You can keep that gruppelberry you're holding, and I can keep this… well, whatever it is,' tapping the 'fruit' as he spoke. Roberto looked down at the gruppelberry his friend had given to him, which was still wet with his own blood. He couldn't exactly refuse this offer, even though it meant every time he spoke to his friend, he would have to see the cause of his wound.

'It's a deal,' he said at last. With that, Geronimo rolled over to the fruit which lay at Roberto's feet, absorbing it into his collection of clippings, and Roberto wiped the magical red fruit as best he could, before putting it back in his pocket. He glanced over at the spiked ball which Geronimo was now trying to crack open by rolling it against a rock. Despite the sharp pain it had caused, his companion's evident joy with this new toy pleased Roberto.

Looking up to the Gothic gargoyles decorating the battlements, he felt that something was watching them. Probably not the gargoyles themselves, since they were clearly made of stone, (though their static glare was certainly daunting) but it seemed that some distant force was following their movements. Geronimo, meanwhile, was trying to convince the other two to go inside the cavernous front door. Albert and Roberto were hesitant, considering the event that had just unfolded, but eventually they acquiesced to Geronimo's insistence.

The thick air inside the hall was moist; bats squeaked above, and their steps echoed off into the distant dark. The castle's former grandeur was evident in the cracked stained-glass windows depicting the royalty and their subjects. In one window, they could see an ominous black dog biting the leg of what appeared to be a soldier, though the window was broken at the top, meaning the face remained unknown.

Roberto admired it for a while, reflecting on the chronic anonymity of war. The seething masses of individuals, each with their own dreams and aspirations, melted together into one faceless crowd, with the hope of ridding the earth of another group of equally powerless young men - themselves similarly coerced into a surreal fight for dominance. His gaze now shifted to the dog; its eyes bulging, lips snarled, veins protruding from its neck. What had caused this rage? Was the dog fighting alone? Was it perhaps even defending itself?

Albert noticed Roberto's silent stare and explained to him how the dog was another spirit of the island. It had lived in this forest since long before the Queens' reign, which enraged Belén, who felt menaced by the dog's authority over the animals and nature there.

'But was the dog good or bad?' Roberto asked. Albert thought about it for a moment.

'Nothing is ever as black and white as good or bad. This spirit did good deeds, like caring for the animals who lived in the forest, yet bad actions too, like what you see depicted here. Remember, this image was made by humans, who probably misunderstood the beast's defence, casting him forever as the villain. Remember - history is always written by the victor.'

The next room was even more lavishly decorated, with tattered banners painted with deep blue, adorned with a shining gold trim hung from the ceiling. A long wooden table stretched across the centre of the chamber, and on it lay silver cutlery and crockery. Though slightly dulled by time, they were still shining with an other-worldly beauty. Intricate carvings embellished their edges, and, at the head of the table lay the grandest of all these items - a great chalice dressed in emeralds, diamonds, and rubies.

The late evening light shone through the empty window frame. It reflected out from these multicoloured stones, still bright as ever despite the tarnished silver they were set upon. A large rat then revealed its head from within, and froze when it saw Roberto. For that moment, Roberto felt ashamed to be human. Its small eyes dilated, its pulse quickened, and it ran fearfully away into a darkened corner. It seemed it had seen humans before, though not in a pleasant situation.

Roberto thought of his mother, who feared rodents more than death itself, who filled their home each winter with traps of all shapes and sizes, lecturing Roberto on how these dirty creatures carried plagues and diseases. For that short moment where their eyes met, it was instead this rat who was filled with the fear of God.

At the opposite end of the room, there stood two tall doors, gilded with gold and resplendent with ornate carvings. On the right, a white goat, on the left, a black sheep. The crowns that hung above their heads showed that these two animals represented royalty. Most likely, they were the Two Queens, and the elegant crests into which these two animals were placed were both decorated with flowers and leaves.

Below them were two words written in some language which Roberto did not understand. The letters were made of sharp curves and quick lines, and were rather beautiful in their own way. Roberto asked Albert if he knew what it said, but he just told him that this language had been lost to time, and that no one could speak it anymore.

'Perhaps someone out there might be able to read it, but this language has not been schpoken for centuries,' Albert added.

Roberto pushed against the cool, shining surface of the right-hand door. It was locked. A large keyhole occupied the centrepiece of the door. The dust which had settled upon the crevices within its ornamented front showed that it had not been opened for a long, long, time.

'Perhaps some key out there might be able to unlock it, but this room has not been opened for many centuries,' Albert chirped in again.

The air grew heavy within the damp walls of the chamber. They all became aware of the presence of mould and rot in the corners of the hall. Even the vaulted roof seemed like it was closing in on them. Roberto began to feel like they were intruding on some ancient, forbidden knowledge, which, as tempting as it may be to investigate, would only result in more situations like his painful experience earlier on with the fruit.

In fact, the deeper they had come into the shadowy echoes of the castle's black rocks, the more Roberto felt the weight of its history, both glorious and tragic, push down upon him. Geronimo seemed to feel this too, and was the first to suggest that they return to the path. The door was not going to be moving any time soon. The room could keep its secrets.

III
Bokoro

Back outside again, the afternoon was drawing a pale pink across the sky. The reclining sun reflected across the tops of wispy clouds stretching throughout the heavens. The animals' quick movements seemed to be slowing as the day wore on, and Roberto began to wonder where they would sleep that night. Albert's tapping feet were a constant reminder that, while they were all free to do *what* they wanted, *when* they wanted, as *slowly* as they wanted, all around them, time was still passing swiftly by.

The sun appeared to be moving at a different speed than the one Roberto was used to at home. He felt as if this day had already lasted for twice as long as normal, yet, at the same time, it felt like dawn had only just blossomed into day. They walked once more beneath the shadow of the dark-fruit-laden tree. Roberto looked down at Geronimo, who still proudly carried the spiny shell on his front. He had long since stopped playing with it, and was now thoroughly distracted by the pink flower freshly picked from the bed beside. The solemn statues overhead watched them from a time long passed. Roberto felt as though they were holding some silent council above, whispering glares to each other from their long, crooked faces.

When there it went! The moment Roberto's eyes turned to the left side of the stone battlements, the lefternmost statue just upped sticks (or, rather, stones) and flew off. Though it was hard to see this dark figure against the light of the sun, it looked very much like the shape of the wise old Alfred.

'Again, I'm sure he would have said a Hoo-llo at least,' thought Roberto to himself. As soon as it had appeared however, it was gone, beyond the wall and off into the North. Neither of his companions appeared to notice this shape at all; Geronimo still playing with the flowers, Albert engrossed in a miniature battle unfolding between two rival colonies of ants.

Waves of tiny sentinels would march forward to meet their inevitable end. The lucky ones being picked up by their compatriots, hoisting injured bodies - squirming in pain - on their backs to be carried home. In the short time that Albert had been admiring this sport, cheering - 'Hurrah! That's it boys! Let 'em have it!' - it seemed that generations of ants had been wiped from existence, and it was now their grandchildren who were emerging from the nest and marching forwards to defeat their rivals.

There was no great patriotism on display here, just defiant duty and dedication to their cause. Soon they would be gone, but thankfully their children were not far behind them, equally ready to defend their colony from their enemy at all costs. Albert, arguably, was the only beneficiary of this cruel sport, for he dutifully picked off any ants who wandered too far from the battlefield, gobbling them up himself as punishment for desertion.

Roberto looked straight ahead of him, through the vaulted arches of the castle's entrance, past the trees, past the darkness, and beyond, into a moment of clarity, where all around him seemed to appear briefly, white. He felt as if he had been sleepwalking and had been suddenly awoken by a bucket of water thrown in his face. His nostrils flared open wide, as a cool breeze flowed across the front of his brain, then down into his lungs. Straight ahead, on the other side of the path, he dreamt of a bridge across the river.

Somehow, despite having followed the river for quite some time, he had not once thought of crossing it. It wasn't a particularly deep river - it was even rather narrow at times - but despite this, the very act of going across to the other side had never occurred to him. Nothing had stopped him doing it, though nothing had particularly encouraged him to go across either. He had understood that there were 'things' over there, more likely than not there would be more of the same animals, more of the same trees, and more of the same clouds above. Yet now, some great desire to see them washed over him.

With this newfound lucidity at the front of his mind, he set off towards its banks. The other two followed him, trying to understand where his silent march was headed.

'We should cross it,' Roberto affirmed when they reached its edge.

Albert nodded his head as he tapped along to the beat of his own footsteps, before asking, 'Where are you headed anyway?' suddenly realising that he had never grasped the reason why their paths had crossed.

Roberto realised he wasn't sure either - until now he hadn't really worried about it. Ever since he was young, he never really had some big, grandiose plan for where he was headed. Everything so far had tended to find its place as he moved forward with his life. Nothing had ever gone too badly wrong in all he had done, but, likewise, it never really seemed to go to the right either.

Geronimo knew where he was going. From the moment he could talk, he had known he exactly where he was going, and where he wanted to be. Roberto hadn't quite worked it out as clearly, nor nearly as quickly, but at least now he'd figured out the direction he was destined to follow.

'I don't know,' Roberto responded at last, 'Though I'm pretty sure it's over there, on the other shore.'

'Y'know, I'd say it might well be that way,' Geronimo piped up, 'We've been following this river for a while now, perhaps it's time that we crossed it - be a good change of scenery, so it would,' Albert nodded silently. 'Aren't you coming with us?' Geronimo asked him.

'Yes, I'm not,' Albert responded, 'I don't belong over there, this side is my home. That foreign air doesn't sit well with me, I've never been able to properly explain myself in that climate. If you wanted, I could take you across in my talons, but your leaves would have to stay here - unless, of course, your friend is willing to carry them.'

Geronimo looked anxiously towards Roberto, who, in turn, looked nervously down at the dark fruit, lying in the tumble of foliage amongst the discarded nuts, the faded tulip, and the ripped rose petals. Roberto, for better or for worse, did not hold any sentimental baggage that he could not carry across, and he quietly thought how the clippings would all wither away at some point anyway. Perhaps it would be better to leave them there, where they had once called home.

Nevertheless, he agreed to carry across what he could, and Geronimo graciously accepted this offer. Albert grasped the small creature in his claws and set off to the other side, leaving Roberto to collect what he could from Geronimo's pile. He was careful not to touch the dark fruit, or any other thorns or nettles that he found there. He clambered onto the mossy rocks that were scattered between where he stood, and where he was going. Some of the leaves were blown out of his arms, being quickly swept away with the bubbles and twigs of that strange river which ran in reverse.

About half-way across, Albert passed him, making his return journey, calling, 'I'll see you again, sometime.' Before disappearing back into the wood. Roberto stopped for a moment to admire the bird's exotic tail-feathers in flight, but moved quickly on, since his feet were growing damp from the excited splashes of the jumping water below.

Geronimo was there, on the bank, already fumbling with some new plants he had found, and by the time Roberto reached the other side, he had already gathered two leaves, a nut, and a small yellow flower. These were soon reunited with the rest of the items Roberto had carried, and they looked around to see that this new place was pretty much like where they had come from.

However, instead of a castle before them, there lay a dilapilumpidated stone path, twisting through the bushes ahead. *[dilapilumpidated; adjective: used to describe a man-made structure (see; bridge, road, &c.) which has been distorted by tree roots.]*

Naturally, they followed it. The trees on this side were mostly the same as the sweet-smelling pines they had seen before, but here, they were organised into neat lines along the edge of the cracked rubble path. Each tree was neatly planted, and spaced out just enough to let their heavy heads reach towards the sun. The lowest branches reached to meet their opposing neighbours with gentle curved handshakes, reminding Roberto of the cavernous halls of the castle. Squirrels jumped athletically here-and-there. The sun had reached that time in the early evening where it shines at its most goldenest, illuminating the sculpted pale trunks of amber timber.

Soon, the path began to rise, curling upwards into the walls of stone that grew from the ground. These in turn lifted them into the treetops, the path cutting back on itself several times as it climbed, leaving the pair positioned directly above where they had previously been. Geronimo lagged behind, trailing Roberto by several steps - more now - given how steep the path was becoming.

The hill was growing into a mountain as they clambered up it. As soon as they felt close to its peak, its elusive zenith would be pushed further away by another stretch of rocks. Many times he wondered why they had started to climb it, instead of attempting to find a way around it. Yet, he never told Geronimo this, since they had come so far already, and it would be a shame not to find out what awaited them on top.

The forest began to grow thin, though some trees managed to cling to the unforgiving stone precipice, their wispy roots poking out from the shallow cracked soil. A flat, shifting sea of green stretched out before them now, disturbed only by the castle's black battlements. The mass of green fell away when it reached the sea, a tall wall of sparkling blue, breaking the trees from the horizon. Occasionally, when he stopped to wait for Geronimo, Roberto could feel the breeze cool the sweat which stuck to his forehead.

They came to a plateau; at its centre stood a lone tall pine, flat-topped and windswept, leaning slightly to the left. At its base there lay a small cluster of sticks leaning against the trunk, cobbled together from the branches that had fallen from this ancient tree, covered all over with a sheet of fine needles.

Off in the distance, sparks of lightning were flying through the sky, but the evening remained quiet. The clattering light was not followed by any rumblings of thunder. Indeed, this strange glow seemed more like a faraway lighthouse shining across the silent landscape, than the tempestuous foreshadowing of a storm.

Despite the lack of materials to light a small fire, Roberto soon realised that it wasn't *really* necessary - the evening was fair, bordering on humid, and the short, quick gusts of fresh sea air made for welcome relief. They sat there for some time in silence, watching the domed heavens above them shift excitedly from shades of gold, to hued pinks, before finally settling into a dark navy blue, slowly filling the sky as the last embers of sun fizzled into the sea.

The flashing lights in the distance shone out more clearly now, sharply contrasted against the dim of the pale night. They could see that they were emanating from another hilltop, not too far off.

With the sun now hidden, and all around them dark, their eyes began to feel heavy, so they went underneath the small shelter around the tree, taking refuge from the misty dew that was beginning to descend from the stars. Not long afterwards, they drifted off into sleep, Roberto propping up his head on his arm, Geronimo pushing himself down into the soft pile of leaves.

Roberto fell into a deep trance, his body pulling down toward the earth, his mind drifting upward like a plume of smoke. His whole world became deathly quiet, even the wind had stopped. Memories of places he had seen, faces he had known, lives he had lived, all appeared before him. Chants of laughter and rumours of speech babbled and boiled in his ears.

At first, these sensations that greeted him seemed rather distant, yet, he felt in his heart that they were once extremely important to him. Now however, he accepted that this crowd of memories was of little use, each of them was a foreign feeling from a time long since passed. He searched among the faces for one which held a deeper meaning than some one-time acquaintance or old schoolteacher, though his mind continued to simply reproduce a torrent of thoughts, ready to be forgotten.

He wasn't sure what exactly he was searching for, though he took comfort in the fact that at least he knew he would recognise it, when he saw it. After all, isn't that the best we can hope for?

These words slowly exposed themselves in his thoughts, bubbling up lethargically before dying away again, echoing in the darkness. They soothed his stress, whilst hushing the encompassing crowd's anxious whispers. Casting his glance towards this group of varied guests, he noticed a small dark face he did not recognise, half-covered by a veil. Though the eyes looked up for just a moment before she turned away, their gaze lingered longer, engrained deeply upon Roberto's mind – so clearly in fact, that it was as if they had been carved there by a curved obsidian blade. Every other face now faded from his memory, leaving only the crudely sketched edges of her face, the impressions of her thin, sharp cheeks, and those eyes.

Those bright pools shone out from beyond time itself, two white nebulas with dense orbs of deep black infinity at their core, more vast than a universe and yet somehow still light and playful. In them, lived the same beauty that has existed since Venus herself fell into the heavens, the harsh contrast of black and white serving only to intensify the twin colours. This vision cut him to the quick, in that moment, he had forgotten all else which had surrounded him. Soon enough, she too was gone, and Roberto drifted back into the long darkness where he lost himself. In this solitude, in this abyss, he felt he had fallen into the midst of her dark eyes. A flash of light and a ringing in his ears.

The breeze was a particularly fresh one that morning, like waking just before dawn, to enjoy the coolest part of the day after a hot summer night. Roberto awoke to see two *real* dark eyes gazing down from above, heavily set, and sombre against the needles and twigs thinly covering the pale blue sky. He recoiled slightly, and heard a looming voice speak from all around him.

'You're awake, I see,' it grunted, as the whole shelter shivered. Geronimo stirred from his slumber, opening his small bright eyes, and looking round. The other pair of eyes above them chuckled and grew soft when it saw Geronimo's surprise.

'Who are you?' Geronimo asked.

'I'm the one that gave you shelter - a thank you would suffice for that alone!' it replied sternly. Intently, it peered at each of the two travellers from what they had thought were eyes, but were in fact two dark wooden knots, set within a pair of branches.

'Well I'm Geronimo!' Roberto heard beside him, the 'eyes' moving back towards the right.

'Hmm, an interesting name. And you?' it said as it turned back to Roberto, coughing slightly as it did so. He said it.

'Ah, a very bright name indeed,' came the response. There followed an expectant silence, but when they eventually realised that no introduction from this new creature was forthcoming, Roberto asked it again,

'Who are you?'

'I am Bokoro, the spirit of this mountain,' it rattled, the eyes shifting down to either side of the door to get a closer look at the pair.

'Ah, good! We were just looking for a mountain!' Geronimo said cheerfully, 'Perhaps you might know it?'

Bokoro frowned, 'I know many mountains. Be more specific, young one.'

'Emm, I don't know much more than that. Apparently, we'll know it, when we see it.'

'Then to see it, you must search for it.'

Geronimo seemed bemused by this roundabout conversation, but at least now they knew what a mountain looked like.

'Do you plan on staying here long?' the woody shape grumbled 'It's just, I have to get going to a cave down this way,' rolling its eyes to the left, 'Some new serow have moved in, and I must check that they are settling in nicely.'

'Oh no,' Roberto replied politely, 'we'll be off soon.'

'Excellent, then I wish you a safe onward journey, and feel free to rest a while up here, but I must be off… Good morning!' The short stack of sticks shook itself free from the tree, shuffling left to right as it closed up the gap that the pair had entered through, like two shutters on a window, and scuttled off down the hillside. Roberto & Geronimo, now left bathing in the warmth of sunshine, watched Bokoro's twigs kick up small stones and dust as it descended into the forest on the other side from where they had climbed up.

'Geronimo, what on earth is a serow?'

'Not a clue. Though I guess we'll find out soon enough.'

Roberto stood to gaze off into the countryside which spread out into the distance. In spite of all the miles they had walked from the sea, and despite the height they had climbed vertically on this mountainside, he began to appreciate how much further they would have to go.

Undulating hills rolled off towards the curved horizon, where the sea on the other side of the island fell behind misty mountains growing where the forest ended. Wide, gentle, and grand, they dominated the skyline, and there, nestled at their centre, was a snow-dusted mountaintop. Sharp as a knife, it cleaved the range in two, its stony symmetrical sides standing tall amongst the soft slopes around it. Geronimo rolled towards the north to view it also, before saying,

'This is surely the one that Alfred and the fisherman were talking about! But just look at it! It's as steep as a cliff! How on earth could he expect me to climb something like that?'

'Did he ever say such a thing? I thought all we had to do was *reach* the top, which is a much easier task than *climbing* to the top.' Roberto gazed at the jagged peak which clambered up, up into the clouds, piercing them and protruding out from their rooves.

Despite what he had just said, Roberto knew that their task – in its current state, might I add– would be impossible. In saying that, he equally knew that they had only just begun! Yes, this spike lay ahead, but below them, in the depths of the valley, flames flickered, and their smoke curled high above the morning mist. As the dew rose, the thick brown woody swirls appeared, as the kindling of fires newly lighted. Some town in the valley was beginning its day, and the people too were beginning their works. But what works? What exactly was there to do in a town on the road from nowhere towards who knows where?

'I suppose we'll find out soon enough.' Geronimo said through the silence. Roberto, taken aback, asked,

'Did I speak? Or are you copying Alfred now?'

'I don't think you spoke, but I could read everything you said. When you know how, it's not very difficult to tell what people are thinking, it's all right there on your face. I think, as Descartes said, it's called philosophy. Or psychology. Or philology. Or physiology. Maybe, it's a little bit of all of them.'

'It seems like we've learned a lot overnight, eh?' said Roberto. Geronimo nodded in agreement, but was somewhat shocked at all the words he had just used. He didn't know what a single one meant. They were apparently correct, since Roberto seemed to understand what had been said, even if they made no sense to he who had spoken them.

'Anyway,' Geronimo thought, 'I can always look them up in a dictionary later. But what was that? What is a dictionary? I know that 'diction' stemmed originally from the Latin, 'dictum' – to speak, and Pictionary is a type of game played by people around Christmas time, so it must be some sort of a speaking game. What is Christmas? What is a game? Oh well. It must be something to do with words. It always is.'

Roberto watched on, as the eyes of his friend screwed up and relaxed repeatedly as all these thoughts ran through Geronimo's mind. He tried to understand what this egg was thinking about, but it only served to make him confused, and judging by the look on Geronimo's face, he quite rightly assumed that his friend was as confused as he was.

Roberto turned back to look at the world which was stretching into life out below them. With the growing light, he could now see a network of connected stone fences that stretched out across the hills, wandering away into the distance. It made him think of olden days, when patient people had generations of time to construct impressive and beautiful things that began years before they were born, and would not end until eons after they had passed. Way off, beyond the pointed mountain, these walls continued, and beside them, trails of ant-like creatures were edging forward together like a snake. Roberto squinted at the distant shapes for a while, before realising that they were other people! With arms, and legs, and heads like his! They still seemed far off, but looking back, seeing how much ground they managed to cover throughout the previous day, he was certain they would reach those cobbled walls before sunset that evening. The pair looked at each other, and they both understood the thoughts passing through the others mind.

'Shall we go?' Roberto asked, and 'Of course,' came the reply. And just like that, they started off down the hill, searching for stable ground to cling to as they went. The path, so carefully constructed on the other side, now crumbled and rolled in lumps down the hillside, worn away by the passing of time, or the passing of feet - it wasn't totally clear which of these was responsible. The plants too, unordered and uneven, clawed their way through the ground, cracking the stones with the vice-grip of their roots. It seemed that that the closer they came to civilisation, the land was putting more and more effort into fighting back against the paving slabs placed upon it.

As the path wound to-and-fro, back and forth, pêle-mêle down to earth, they passed the cave which Bokoro had mentioned before taking leave of them. Within it there there lay a stag and a nanny goat huddled around their kid – a serow, I suppose we'll call it – who was struggling to stand. Its thin legs shook and collapsed under its own weight.

Bokoro stayed close by, almost showing concern in its stoic knotted eyes as it watched the pathetic child push itself to its extremes, before inevitably crumpling to the floor. The bundle of branches seemed confused by the creature's inability to complete such a simple action. Roberto & Geronimo peered in at the scene which unfolded before them, before Roberto moved toward them, turning to Bokoro.

'Give me a few of your sticks,' he said.
Bokoro, shocked, asked him, 'What for?'
'Just trust me.'

Bokoro was made visibly uncomfortable by this – after all, they were *Bokoro's* sticks – but it nonetheless acquiesced to the demand. Roberto kneeled down, and untied his shoes. Picking up the few twigs that were left to him, he moved with care near to the baby, its wide eyes growing large with fright, for it had likely never seen a human before. Taking his pocket-knife, and cutting his laces in two, he made four lengths of white strings, silver metal tips at their ends. Roberto stretched the shoelaces, and took the serow's weak front legs, tying them to the sticks.

The serow stood, awkwardly at first, trying its hardest to bend its front knees in line with the straight twigs, and relieving some of the weight it carried using its hind legs. The young creature lifted its head proudly. The parents, wide-eyed and bushy-tailed, gave a look of thanks, but said not a word.

Roberto & Geronimo took their leave of this tranquil scene, making their way down the mountain towards the valley's basin. When they got to the bottom, they saw a small dark pool that had been carved out by a short waterfall. Its hard rock edges as sharp as knives, thick moss creeping up from the waters below. The rushing stream bubbled as it hit the mirrored surface, creating dazzling mists which turned to rainbows as they bounced in the sunlight. Fresh air filled their noses, making their heads swirl after the descent.

A heavy-looking bird, white as snow, flew by. Roberto wondered how its thin wings managed to keep it up there. Following its path, he noticed it was flying along a canal, a sort of rough, brown-edged channel that led off towards where they had seen the walls beforehand. Staring at it in awe, he was amazed it had the strength to push itself so rhythmically, so carefully away from the ground, then his trance was broken by Geronimo jumping.

'There's something in the water!' Geronimo shouted, watching the spot from whence a wide ripple grew - larger than a fish at its edges, yet smaller at its core than an insect. When Roberto looked however, he could see nothing in the emerald stream, and suggested they move on. He never quite escaped the feeling that he was being watched by some distant eyes from deep within its jewelled waters.

END OF VOLUME ONE

...mountains of clouds,

...skies of seas,

...isles of stars,

...rains of rocks

VOLUME TWO

IV
Tamna Town

V
Les Orageistes

VI
Ejército Zapotec

DEUXIÈME PARTIE

IV
Tamna Town

And so, they walked on.

The channel was not nearly as beautiful as the river on the other side of the mountain. Its banks were straight, steep, and had clearly been carved out with many men's spades. Trees were neatly planted in long lines stretching away from it, but their fruit seemed too large and unnatural for the crooked grey branches that held them. Long stalks of yellow grass reached up and over chunks of dead wood, making the whole place feel like it was once loved and cared for, but not for many years. Eventually, the long grass they were pushing down as they walked became a rough path covered in brown gravel, and simple fences divided the fields into farms. In the distance, where the trees faded into the sky, a faint light grew, becoming at first a flicker, then a flame, and finally, a man carrying a torch.

Slowly he trudged onward, not noticing Roberto & Geronimo. The boy's long khaki shorts and Geronimo's light shade of green made them hard to spot in the morning's mist. For the guard, this was no more than another day's work, where he was paid handsomely to wake before sunrise on the early shift. Almost always he had had little to report back, except for one time - where a boy had gone missing out in the woods, and was found three days later, having gotten stuck behind a boulder in a cave he had crawled into. This was about to change.

Today, he looked up the long straight canal, towards the gentle peak of the mountain ahead, to see two of the strangest figures he had ever seen.

Well, one of the strangest in any case. Roberto looked much like any other boy in his town, yet somewhat more exotic. No, it was Geronimo rolling forward, light as air, peering up from his plump pillow, who was new to him. While he might normally have jumped back, or even straightened his back (like when you're trying to scare off a bear), the man just stood there, frozen, but at ease.

It was soon obvious to him that these unusual travellers meant no harm, and he smiled while stretching out his hand. The glow of his torch cut through the muggy air, now shining fully on their faces.
'Haii!' he said at last. This greeting was very loud, compared with the short 'Heyi!' that Roberto responded with, yet they both clearly understood each other.

And there they stood for a time, smiling and shaking hands, making themselves appear as friendly and harmless as possible, without another word being said between them.

'Garuda!' he shouted after this brief interlude, turning his thumb to point towards his chest, smiling as hard as he could.

'Roberto' he responded, repeating the gesture, puffing out his chest proudly as he said it. Garuda nodded in understanding, but seemed to have trouble with the pronunciation. After a few failed attempts – 'Romero' 'Rodrigo' 'Ropato' – to name but a few – he eventually grasped it. He turned his eyes downward to Geronimo who was trying to copy this manner of introduction, yet struggling with his lack of opposable (or any) thumbs. Besides, Geronimo considered it rather rude to point (quite rightly!).

Garuda gestured to follow him back in the direction from whence he had come. They followed him, grateful not to arrive as complete strangers to a town, especially when they did not speak the language. Moving quicker now on the hastily pebbled path, they passed Garuda's fellow sentries, who stopped and stared at his new companions - finding them just as strange as he had. Before long, a few wooden buildings came into view up ahead.

'Tamnah!' said Garuda, pointing at the hamlet nestled between the mountains' narrow walls. The people there were just starting to awake; kettles were boiling, spoons were clanging on copper pans, and ladies were carrying baskets of food from the store. There were fresh fruits of all varieties, thick loaves, and creamy milk for porridge.

Tamna Town, as they understood it to be called, must have had only three hundred odd residents, give or take the few who didn't seem quite so odd to Roberto. There were even a couple of boys around his age, feeding their dogs as they walked along the muddy main street of the town. This street curved round on itself in a semicircle, leading at either end to two sturdy wooden bridges across the rushing river, where they could see more wooden houses built right the way up the steep mountainside.

Garuda smiled and waved to the people, seemingly unaware that they weren't looking at him, as they slowly appeared from their houses to get a look at the strange visitors he accompanied. Geronimo tried to hide behind Roberto's leg, never having seen such a large group of humans before. Roberto was nervous too, for he had never been regarded with such curiosity back home, yet here, his appearance seemed awfully foreign to everyone around him. Garuda, on the other hand, seemed quite well pleased with all these eyes upon him, appearing annoyed when their gaze shifted to admire what he'd found, rather than him, for what he'd achieved. Which, all things considered, was not much. Unlike the heroes and soldiers of old, he had not had to fight a wild beast, or slay a large dragon, he had simply found two wandering travellers - not much of a feat.

Up they marched to the doors of the largest building, where guards - most of them taller than Garuda, but bearing the same crest and armour - glared distrustfully at the pair as they entered the low wooden hall. Roberto felt the room had been deliberately built smaller than it should have been, to make the guards outside seem more intimidating. At the end, at a wide wooden desk, sat a wide little man with a feather in his hat. He was busy writing letters with his left hand, and stamping envelopes with his right. Roberto was surprised at how busy the man appeared to be, for, where Roberto came from, important-looking men at desks only ever pretended to be busy - and it took them a long time doing that too.

Ruddy-faced and flustered, he looked up from the documents he was signing, to view the trio advancing towards him. Pushing back his little spectacles, he closed another letter. He slid it towards an attendant, who passed it to another, who then walked off to give it to someone else.

A snooty clerk moved forward, asking, 'What is your business? Can't you see that the Mayor is very busy? Have you an appointm…'

'What do you want?' the Mayor grunted sternly, making all who were present jump slightly. Garuda stood to attention and began speaking in his strange foreign tongue, with the Mayor nodding along as he listened. He then turned back to Roberto, and addressed him in a matter-of-fact manner.

'I'm very sorry sir, but our tourism office has been closed for over a year. As you can imagine, we don't receive a great many travellers, away out here. However, as a token of appreciation for your visit today, I would like to offer you a voucher for a free loaf of bread from the pride of Tamna Town - our bakery, which you will find just next door. Now, if you will kindly excuse me, I have a lot of ink to stamp, and ordinances to enact, so I do hope you will enjoy your time here with us… Good morning!' he tipped his round hat and continued writing notes and handing them to his assistants. Before they had reached the door, the pair were given two papers marked with strange writing and pictures of bread by one of the clerks bustling around, sorting papers and straightening pens.

Back outside again, Roberto & Geronimo thought that another small group had gathered to look at them, but were instead crowding into the entrance of the neighbouring bakery.

As quickly as light had filled his sight, they were brought inside and up to the counter. The dust inside made Roberto sneeze, swiftly followed by the bright daze which accompanies changes of scenery. As his eyes strained once again to adjust to the dark, Roberto saw the bakers, four in all, working away.

They appeared to be a family, father working the flames, mother rolling the dough, a son, slightly older than Roberto, working in several places at once... and a daughter. At first glance she seemed younger than Roberto, yet when he looked more closely, her face seemed as if it had lived for a hundred lifetimes already – so much so that Roberto felt he was looking into her future, as much as her past, or even her present.

It was to her that Garuda spoke, still acting as their guide, though her distant eyes would drift down to meet Roberto's own. She looked at the two vouchers and sighed. Calling out a strange assortment of words to the rest of the family, they all nodded in turn.

Two fresh loaves appeared, were then wrapped up in a large leaf, and placed on the counter by the girl. Roberto did not yet know how to thank someone in the local language of this place, so he nodded, bowed his back, and said 'Thank you' in his own tongue, as that was the only way he knew how. The girl's face lit up when he said this, and it seemed that she had understood him.

'You are welcomed,' she blushed back. Amazed, Roberto asked if the girl could show him around the town, since no-one else except the unfriendly mayor had spoken in a way he could comprehend.

'Can't now, but finish work at high sun. Come back then,' she smiled softly and turned to face another customer.

Excited, Roberto checked the sun as he went back outside. It was now reaching over the rooftops and lying just behind the trees at the end of the valley. The town was situated along a straight glen with a river at its basin, angled perfectly to receive the sun's rays throughout the day, rising at one end before setting in the other. They had some time to spend before the sun would reach its apex, so they walked, with Garuda greeting the crowds on their behalf. Round and round they went, on the sole rough circular path which led around the town, crossing over the bridge to the opposing, residential side, before the path looped round on itself again to meet the other bridge.

Life seemed to move at a different pace here, compared with what Roberto was used to. In his country, people were always running late, doing lots and driving themselves crazy. Here, everyone just walked. Granted, the short donkeys would sometimes be seen to trot on occasion, though always leisurely and at their own pace, never being driven by their masters. It was surprising that the Mayor seemed so busy, since all of his ordinances weren't exactly being enacted quickly. Even the bakers, who were the fastest-moving folk he had seen, made such efficient and natural movements that they never appeared to be as flustered as the Mayor was as he sat at his desk.

At the end of the town, where the trees swayed and sang with robins, there stood a large worn-down tree. It had evidently been the grandest tree in town, but time had worn it away, and now, it was no more than a grey, leafless husk. They learned from Garuda (slowly, and with many hand movements), how the locals had watered it and nurtured it, yet one winter, it simply never grew back in the springtime. That winter, though not especially cold, many of the boys who worked in the city during summer, were not able to make it back during the autumn, and much of the pruning that would then happen as they played and climbed only served to leave it weak and frail. As

Roberto walked up to it, he noticed a small bee. Well, it was small, all things considered, but large for a bee.

Now, there were many other insects around, which Roberto had spent his days waving away as they walked through the forest - so many in fact, that it would be very boring to tell you all about each and every one of them. Yet, he had seen this bee at least *three times* previously. Always, it was hovering gently by him, hiding in bushes, and darting away just when it realised it had been spotted. Ever since he had arrived in San Salvador, he had felt some sort of a gaze gently watch over him. It buzzed off into the treetops above. Roberto turned his head upward, and saw that already the sun was approaching its highest point.

The town was beginning to wind down together for lunch. Savoury spices and salty sweet smells swelled from kitchen windows. They turned back and walked up the opposite side of the street. Roberto & Garuda's stomachs grumbled at the thick chunks of gammon, but Geronimo did not like the smell of it at all. He much preferred the chestnuts that were roasting, or the cool bottles of fruit juices which lay on the market tables. Back at the bakery, there was the usual crowd who were "running late today!" as per usual, buying their sandwiches for lunch. The girl was there, visibly tired, but working even quicker than before, saving her energy for the last stretch, just as good marathon runners always do. She looked happy to see the three of them (Garuda was still there) and as soon as the last customer had been served, she turned confidently and addressed them in quite a formal manner.

'Hello, gentlemen. Hana is my name. You shouldn't go any further without my assistance.' This haughty voice took Roberto by surprise, for he had not yet forgotten the grammatical mistake she made earlier – "You are welcomed."

However, when he thought about it later on, he realised it was in fact he! that was wrong, and Hana had welcomed him to the Tamna Town Bakery.

As it turned out, she had in fact a much better, and nicer-sounding accent than his own, and she enunciated every word clearly and politely. Garuda had, by now, gotten bored, and wandered off somewhere. Presumably, his nose pulled him towards a table for lunch.

The three of them walked on, as Hana told of the town's history. She pointed out that the dark wooden houses were the oldest, carved by hand many moons ago, and the sturdier, thicker-walled mansions were newly built by the General and his Guards, who had arrived only a few decades before. The 'tickets' that the Mayor had written were no more than threats to the bakers, who were 'obliged' by 'public service' to provide rations to the travellers. Hearing this, they felt relieved that they had only eaten an end of the crust, and had saved the bread to eat with Hana, who had brought several sweet jams from the shop. The stroopelfruit-flavoured one was their favourite.

They picnicked beneath the great weary ash tree they had passed earlier. She told them that ever since well-paid jobs in the city had dragged most of the young, able-bodied workers away from Tamna, the trees had all lost their lustre. Greens were brighter way back then, according to their grandmothers (though some say their eyesight has failed, whilst their memories remain as fresh and clear as ever). Back in their day, in late spring, they would hold festivals at Laloo. These began just before the summer's heat when the skies reached their lightest shade of blue, when everyone would go on holiday, down upstream by the ocean.

But the festival building at Laloo had fallen into ruin. Now, where once the joyous celebrations took place, grave, dark stones marked the places where families remembered loved ones of times passed. It was said by some, that long, long ago, there were GIANTS! living on that island! Some of the oldest folk said they had even seen the last two giants up in the hills, though *they* were so old that few people would still listen to the silly things they would say.

Hana, however, was one of these few. Her grandfather (may he rest in peace) swore that he had once met 'Les Orageistes' or 'the storm-bringers' in his youth, atop Mt. Zapateca, where the pair's arguments caused the friction which make the sky spark and crack into thunder.

Before this, the giants had lived closer to Tamna, and had fled to the mountains from the guards of the new government in the city. These guards were not bad people per se, they had merely been the recipients of bad orders from their superiors, who felt menaced by the giant's authority over the weather, and ultimately, the seasons. The giant's house was apparently very large, probably around the size of a cathedral near you, with windows as big as buses, and doors which echo when they were closed. The place was much too big for human habitation, so eventually it grew overgrown with trees. Roberto wondered if these two giants were the same as the Two Queens that Albert had mentioned earlier, as the description of Laloo sounded much like the castle they had passed.

'I'm sure *they* would be able to help you find this mountain,' Hana told them, 'Plus, they're apparently much nicer to strangers than locals, so I'm sure you'd have no problem going up and meeting them.'

'Hold on, what's all this about going up again?' exclaimed Geronimo, before explaining how going uphill was not quite his forte, given his tendency to roll back down.

'Well I'm sorry,' said she - though not in a rude or sarcastic way, 'But sometimes that's how life can be, sometimes it's those trials that make us into the people we are now.' And she was right you know.

After chatting a while, and telling Hana that they must have passed through Laloo in the forest on their way to Tamna, she invited the pair to dine at her house that evening. Naturally, they accepted the offer with more than a little graciousness. Hana said it would take her a few hours to get it ready. Her parents may already have started preparations, and she may need to run to the storehouse to get extras. Roberto & Geronimo watched her adoringly as she walked quickly away from them.

'Boy, she sure was something!' exclaimed Geronimo.

'Yes, she was,' replied Roberto wistfully.

'Can you believe she expects us to climb that mountain?'

'Yet, somehow we knew,' continued Roberto, though it was not clear whether or not he had even heard Geronimo's question. Roberto's head whirled around at a million thoughts per minute, completely smitten by her kindness and her grace. Hospitable folk such as Hana do not come around often, and Roberto knew this. At the same time, however, those deep-gazing eyes from his dreams lingered long in his memory, and he felt them watch him still. They moved from face to face, animal to human, always disappearing just as they came into Roberto's line of sight.

As it was now early evening, the moon rose to join its sister sun in the sky. It seemed to be chasing the sun off towards the horizon, making the weather slightly colder, and the heavens, somewhat cooler. Even up there, somewhere amongst the moon's dusty craters and dry white seas, it felt like an extra-ordinarily large beast was watching from amongst the bleached sands.

The moon moved faster than the sun, which had been strolling rather leisurely in the direction of lunchtime. Yet now, the golden celestial orb was in the slow (on a human scale) rush (on an astronomical scale) towards the far end of the valley, where, nestled like a sapphire, you could just barely see the upper edge of the ocean.

'We'll find a way up,' said Roberto, breaking a long silence. Geronimo looked up at him in disbelief, knowing full well that under current conditions, there was no chance of making it. But something had convinced

Roberto, whispering quietly into the back of his mind, that they could indeed do it. He knew they had not made it this far through luck alone.

The sun struck dinner-time, and the pair suddenly found themselves hungry. They walked back up towards the bakery, as Hana had told them that the family lived together at the rear of it. All the doors to the houses were open, and smells even more vibrant than lunchtime filled the air. In fact, in some houses, it almost seemed as if lunch hadn't stopped, where old men were drinking some foul-smelling beverage, and playing cards with their wrinkled hands. Hammocks hung from the rafters, and wide, wooden platforms kept the old folk, who were sitting cross-legged on the ground, off the ground. There were lots of long, fat pigs wandering around, some with stomachs so large that they almost touched the ground. They weren't so different from normal pigs really, but their faces seemed wiser, and prouder than those in our world.

When they reached the bakery, they knocked three times, and were greeted by Hana's father, who was wearing a comfortable-looking neckerchief, a checked shirt, and a wide hat, holding in his hand a great big onion. He smiled brightly, given he had been expecting them, and greeted them both in his native tongue. Roberto tried to repeat the words, but muddled them up. The man laughed and patted him on the shoulder, evidently appreciating that Roberto had at least made the effort.

He ushered them inside and brought them through a door behind the counter, out into a wide kitchen where the rest of the family were working away preparing the dinner. Their aprons and washcloths were vivid shades of violet, which all swirled in the pale orange of sunset. Each face looked towards them and smiled, but quickly returned to the tasks they were simultaneously performing.

This house was very much like the others they had seen, mostly one large room, with hammocks, sheets, clothes, and many other knitted fabrics, all hanging from the wooden ceiling. Partitions of wood and thin cotton sheets could change the size of the large room, shaping it into several individual rooms, with wooden dividers sliding back and forth on slick varnished floors.

A clean, cool vapour arose from the central fireplace, where a pot of salted water was boiling. Hana came over to greet them, and her brother took over the rolling of the thick yellow paste she had been working with. The father took the place of the son at the counter, continuing chopping the onion he was holding. It seemed they could read each other's minds, and together, they worked as one to create the feast. It was simple, with few flavours - instead offering quality over quantity. Each vegetable, each cut of meat, and each fried piece of dough were able to let their tastes shine through.

They all ate slowly that evening, taking their time to chat in the strange broken creole that marked the mixing of their two distinct languages. When any point was difficult to get across, Hana would step in as a translator of sorts, working as a mediator. The table was low, and they sat down upon the carpet which covered most of the floor. This meant Geronimo was not left on a lower level with the house animals, and joined the conversation on an equal level. Geronimo seemed to have a natural flair for the language of Tamna, picking it up much quicker than Roberto, who had to rely on Hana's interpretations. Still, Roberto learned much of this local speech they called 'Pashtamna'.

The Ririroko family, ('bakers' was pronounced in Pashtamna as 'Reeree-rohkoh') had been running the Tamna Town Bakery for centuries. Their homeplace was known to everyone in the town, for the Ririrokos would often host large dinners for their closest friends and relations. On these evenings, they would pull back all the partitions to let a great table occupy the hall.

Sadly, these meals were now reserved for special occasions like birthdays, which often had less than half of the people who had once gathered there. The family simply did not have the ability to feed so many folk, after the General and his Guards had moved into the ruins which lay on the other side of the valley.

Every day, the mayor would write out meal vouchers for the troops, and every day, the family were obliged to send the majority of their wares away on caravans of mules to the camp in the mountains. All these 'donations' to the 'public interest' had left the town itself with intermittent food shortages, especially on days when the soldiers felt they had worked extra hard, and demanded more food be delivered to their base. This, naturally, had upset the townsfolk, who were not exactly pleased with the orders being given by the distant city's equally distant leaders.

Hana's father, who had watched his wealth be taken from him since he was a boy, harboured a particular dislike for the General who was placed in command of their region, the General Santos. It was he who had ordered the expedition into the ruins where the long dead of Tamna were buried, where none dared enter, under oath to their ancient Queen Hélène.

It was said by their elders that Hélène, who would roam the forests disguised as a black dog, had sealed her sister Belén within. The Two Sisters were said to still watch over the town, dressed as two objects they called the sun, and the moon, respectively. Much like those two stars which burn in the heavens, Bélen was never as bright as her sister, and could only ever be clearly seen when her sister was not around. One of those days, in winter, when Hélène left early to chase animals in the forest (under the guise of the black dog, of course), Belén saw her opportunity, and claimed her sister's bright golden throne, and ordered it to be recast in silver.

Now, if you have ever seen a piece of gold jewellery, you will know that within, you can see a little goldener reflection of yourself, much like how your garden looks on a summer's evening, when the sun takes its time as it nears the horizon.

If you have been lucky enough to have also seen a silver piece of jewellery, you will know that the reflections within are much colder in colour than the gold, yet often reflect a scene exactly as it is. So it was too with the thrones.

When Hélène had returned, and saw her throne covered with silver plates, she flew into a very un-ladylike rage, and sealed her sister to the shining silver throne. This action, done in broad daylight in front of a crowd, made many of the island's residents turn against Hélène. As they saw it, Belén was simply behaving in her usual impish ways, which regularly added much merriment to their lives, and were normally of little *true* harm. Hélène, on the other hand, had behaved erratically, and out of anger, causing a long future of torturous imprisonment - to her own sister!

This was unacceptable to many folk, who, no longer willing to live near Hélène's shrine, had moved long ago out to the western shores, to where the land was drier. However, with a sea so plentiful of fish, it was no longer necessary to plant farms of fruits and vegetables. The settlement prospered and quickly grew, but the people there, according to the Ririrokos, were as coarse as the sandy ground they walked on, and pale as the dusty mud walls which encircled them. There were many types of people in the city, though apart from these ex-Tamna folk, they were mainly divided into two groups, the Astrognomers, and the Falconers.

The Astrognomers are a sort of short type of people. They are natural observers, and pride themselves on their studies of 'astronogy' - which consists of observing the bright parts of the skies, which they believed to be somehow linked to the shiny metals found in underground caverns. Falconers, on the other hand, are much taller, and all things considered, a much quieter bunch. They are interested mainly in the space between the

stars, which is, to them, much more important, since it took up the majority
of the sky above.

The city, known as Ballyna, was always bitter towards the folk who
stayed in Tamna Town. The harvests there were much larger, and the food
was tastier, so they ordered their troops to set up camps nearby, and have the
General's Guard patrol the town. The Mayor of Tamna (himself an
Astrognomer) had until recently been just another paper pusher within the
White Tower at Ballyna.

He had been thrust into this job, and was not really to blame for all
those bread vouchers he had been writing. It was, after all, his job to feed the
troops, and much worse circumstances would await him if he did not
complete his work to the best of his abilities – not to mention the group of
rowdy, hungry young men who would then descend upon the town! It seemed
to the pair that this General Santos was the real problem, for they learnt that
his fanatic admiration of Belén was what had pushed the city's council to
begin their excavation of the ruins, subsequently causing the town's
misfortunes.

Sensing the low spirits that such a serious conversation had evoked,
Hana's mother, Pat, as she was called, signalled to her daughter to join her in
the kitchen. They returned moments later with pots of thick, foaming green
tea, and creamy desserts on a large golden tray. This brightened their moods,
and the conversation was shifted towards the Pashtamna language, their
culture, and the party music they would play on small earthen ocarinas. It was
with these colourful lively occasions in mind that they drifted off to sleep that
night. Pat wouldn't let Roberto & Geronimo go away so easily, having set up
a hammock and moved the partitions around to create a cosy little room for
the pair.

Roberto, however, had a hard time falling asleep that night, as his
mind raced with thoughts of Hana. He had wanted to invite her along with

them, to act as their guide through the mountains, but had so far not gotten up his nerve. After a long while tossing and turning in the cool linen sheet, he quietly got up, carefully creeping past Geronimo, fast asleep, and out onto the back porch.

The chickens were nesting upon a high piece of wood. The variety of rustles and distant rumbles made Roberto think of the creatures he had met, of the fisherman who might be repairing his net, and of all the people in the city he had yet to meet. Suddenly, he heard a noise behind him, and saw Hana creeping through the screen door. She moved almost silently, except for the noise her sandals made as they glided across the wooden floor. There she stood, bathed in moonlight, sweetly gazing up at the stars.

'Could you not sleep?' she asked earnestly.

'No, I had something I wanted to ask you.'
She seemed slightly surprised by this, though at the same time, as if she had been expecting to hear it.

'Oh,' she said, after a moment's silence, knowing precisely what Roberto was about to say, even though he had yet to say it.

'I want you to come with Geronimo and I.'
Hana, who had been gazing at Roberto while he was putting those words together, moved her eyes sadly towards the floor.

'I'd really like to, you know, but…' she trailed off.

'But what?' Roberto replied, noticing his own voice had become strangely aggressive.

'But… I must think of my duties here,' she continued at last, 'They need me to work at the bakery, especially with the food shortages.' She looked up again. 'This is my home. I have grown with it, and my home has grown me. I'd like to have an adventure someday, but the moment just isn't right. Think of all the people that need their bread! Where will they get it from if I just left? My parents would be worked even harder than now, and no doubt would be worn out even sooner without my help! No.' she said, shaking her head. It seemed she was finally saying out loud all the thoughts which had been swirling around her mind throughout the day. 'No, my town needs me, and I must stay.'

Sorrowfully, she looked up at Roberto, hugged him quickly, and went back inside. At first Roberto felt embarrassed for what he had said, before realising that it was completely necessary. At the very least, he knew the answer. If he had not asked, he would never have known. This thought comforted him, and he went back inside to dream of the circular road which ran through the town.

Round and around it went, families being born, families dying, and babies being born again to keep the traditions alive. Sometimes, he grew irritated that they would not change, but in the end, he accepted that they really had no need to.

V
Les Orageistes

Geronimo awoke first that morning.

Looking out from a crack between the planks of the wall, Geronimo saw that outside it was raining, and Tamna Town was waking. Old ladies were collecting clothes to launder, placing them in small wooden carts which they were pulling behind them. Their grandchildren were running in front, knocking on doors and collecting the money. Two-by-two they marched up the street, using large exotic leaves as umbrellas to keep their bright airy dresses from being drenched by the rains. They carried gold and silver pouches beneath their arms, one for the money and one for the receipts, though they did not all seem to be using the same colour of purse for the same purpose.

The rain did not seem like it would hang around. The sun was breaking up the clouds already, creating bright reflections through the rain drops. Turning back to the room, Geronimo saw Roberto was still slumbering deeply, and would not be awake for some time yet, so he decided to get up and see if anyone else was awake.

Nudging back the partitioned wall, and re-closing it behind him, Geronimo moved down the hall towards the end with the fire pit. Finding no-one, he went out through the back doors, where he could hear noises echoing in the backyard.

Outside were Hana's father and brother, pouring grain from metallic buckets to feed their menagerie of animals. The father and the brother smiled and waved, beckoning Geronimo to come forward. He clambered awkwardly down the stairs towards them, and across the short yard to where the sheds were. Geronimo had yet to see so many animals packed together in one place in his short life, and these farmyard beasts were quite strange and scary to him.

Four-legged heaps of meat stood above, three times his height, and twice as wide, looking down over their noses, both eyes trained on Geronimo. One of them stuck out its tongue and licked Geronimo's face. He didn't like that. The men laughed, before telling him not to worry, that the 'lamna' as these creatures were called, were only tasting to see if Geronimo was ripe yet. He was not.

The men pointed to some other animals, the 'bamna' which were much sturdier creatures, and the 'gamna' which were much smaller, with pointed mouths, and stood on high perches, making loud squawks.

Geronimo could understand even more of the local language than the previous evening, and was able to politely thank the father for his hospitality, which he appreciated all the more to hear spoken in his own tongue. As a token of their friendship, and to save Geronimo the hardship of toiling up the mountain, Matt, as the father was known to his close friends and relations, offered one of his lamna as a gift to Geronimo.

'They're good to ride on, and their long necks have perfect balance, so you won't even notice the incline.' He explained in Pashtamna. The thought of this very much pleased Geronimo, even if it would mean once again leaving his pile of hard-won leaves behind. For the moment though, he did not worry, it was still too early to leave, and anyway, Roberto was not yet awake. Mother Pat had appeared at the back door, waving at her boys to come inside for their breakfasts. Geronimo came along to join their table, but wasn't very hungry, and ate only a few nuts. Soon the family left, kindly excusing themselves to help out Hana, who was working alone until the point in the morning when the bakery began to get busier.

Geronimo took the opportunity to try out the new lamna, and went for a stroll around town, hanging from a small woollen pouch which Ma (as Pat was also known) had knitted and slung around the creature's pointed ears which looked almost like horns. It could not speak, which disappointed Geronimo, as he had only ever met talking animals like Alfred & Albert, He had, by now, become rather adept at speaking Pashtamna, and so, was directing his conversation towards passers-by, all of whom seemed amazed by the new contraption which this strange little thing had contrived for himself.

For a few hours, they walked around on that one circular street, stopping at times to talk with the working ladies and young boys who rode on the back of lamna, with colourful ropes and woollen bags hanging from their saddles.

Geronimo had been enjoying this newfound freedom so much that he did not notice the time, and realised that it was almost half-way to midsun! The day was getting along, and he should probably go back and find Roberto!

This they did, passing the crowded front of the bakery, and sidling up its narrow alleyway to the rear courtyard. Even from outside, he could still clearly hear the sound of Roberto snoring, and went in to wake him. Geronimo hopped out of his lamnapsack, and, getting back into his little nest which he had neatly swept behind the door earlier, he nudged Roberto's back through the hammock.

This pushed him out of his slumber, and onto the ground below, where he murmured something and looked around confusedly, as he re-joined real life once more. Geronimo hadn't meant to make him fall, but still found the sight somewhat amusing, and had to apologise for not holding back a laugh. Roberto had been in the midst of an uneasy dream, and his eyes were dazzled by the escalating sun which now poked through the gaps in the thatched roof.

Guilt creeped over him, for he had woken much earlier, before even Geronimo, but had turned over again (though he never told Geronimo this, despite his friend's teasing for his laziness). He knew it would be a long road up through the mountains, especially if the path was paved by giants - who normally use bumpy and uneven hexagon tiles for their roads, instead of flat squares or tarmac like we would use. At length, he stirred, got himself ready, and pulled back the partition. The bakery seemed less busy than the previous day, and Ma Pat had retired early to the living quarters, preparing dishes and repurposing fabrics into bags and coats for Roberto & Geronimo.

There was enough food on the table to feed a dozen for several days, but Ma insisted the pair took it all, for they could well get stuck up in the mountains. Besides, it wouldn't weigh the lamna down at all - they were used to carrying these sorts of provisions, and the one Geronimo had received was good and strong, in the prime of his years. They gladly accepted her kindness, and got themselves ready to go – though not before lunch, which Ma insisted they eat before leaving.

'Always take a hot meal when it's offered to you!' she said.

The bakery crowds were winding down, and metal cutlery was clinking on tables throughout the town. Once again, merry echoing laughs heralded the height of sun and the coming of midday meals. Roberto and Geronimo helped with setting the table and stirring the pots, before the rest of the family joined them in the back room. First to arrive were the father and brother, followed shortly after by Hana. She seemed shyer than before, hardly daring to look at Roberto, instead playing with Geronimo on the floor. She knew this would be the last time she would ever see the pair.

A certain sadness lingered over her face, even when she smiled at Geronimo's jokes. It pained Roberto to see this, yet there was nothing that could be done. Later on, when he was alone with his thoughts and memories, he grew glad that he had met her, even if her sweet memory had faded significantly.

For the moment however, he spent his last moments with Hana admiring her movements. Her long, thin fingers drew back her long, black hair to show her golden earrings. Her wide moist eyes were fixed downwards at Geronimo's leaves, and her muscat perfume drifted across the table to meet Roberto's nose. He savoured these few tender memories for a long time afterwards.

Over the meal, Hana's father, Matt, explained how they should go 'Mauka' a strange word which Hana said could not be translated directly. It was a word which meant 'away from the sea' or 'towards the mountains,' for in Pashtamna they did not use directions like left and right, or compass points like north and south.

They simply had no need. They never ventured too far from their homes, and, if they did, it was probably towards the sea, which they described as going 'Makai.' These strange directions were always easy to work out on the fly however, for both the mountains and sea were visible from all places on the island. Besides, since the wind always blew in from the sea, you would only have to follow it to find your way again.

After dining, or rather, lunching, it was time to begin their journey. Such a pilgrimage up the sacred mountain of storms was known in Pashtamna as an 'echtra'. Although he was sad to leave, Roberto kept finding the phrase, 'That's the way!' swirling around in his mind, which made his departure sting a little less. That really was, just the way – people come just as quickly as people go, and we should always try and take some comfort in that.

Their stomachs filled, they said their goodbyes, and went down into the street. They passed the tree, and went up through the wild hedges towards the mauka end of the valley. Looking back, they saw the Ririroko family gazing thoughtfully up towards them. Even if he knew in his heart of hearts he would never see them again, Roberto still felt obliged to repay their kindness somehow, and his mind turned to this 'General Santos' who had suppressed them.

Quickly though, his thoughts turned back to the uneven ground which they walked upon, covered with brambles and thorns growing up through broken rocks. Up and up it climbed, quite steeply now, until they were passing the heights of the treetops of Tamna.

At the top of the valley, they came to a wide open plain, which was populated only by the few adventurous trees who dared climb up so high. There were still a few farms up here, in the upper valley's floor, where they saw many smaller fruits growing on wispy, weedy branches. Steep stone steps had been carved into the rocks, letting a few young boys with wide hats trot along on their horses – though they were not quite horses as you might know them. Rather, they were short and stubby little horses, with wide hooves to keep them stable on the crumbling, dusty hillside. 'Konies' they called them.

The river was much thinner up here, and the land looked thirstier. There remained but a trickle of stream, and little life around to drink from it. Still, they followed it upwards, passing tall trees with pointed ends which had set up camp beside the weak flow of water. They crossed this wasteland for some hours without encountering anything remarkable at all. Sometimes, our journeys can take us through these sorts of empty spaces and quiet places, and that's ok.

A few hours had passed by, by the time they reached the other side. The once powerful gush of water now stood almost completely still, settling into pools of clear, mirrorlike reflections.

The sun was now setting, and the pair agreed to set up their tent beside a wide, clear lake. They did not talk to each other much that day, simply preferring to be alone with their thoughts and the whistling winds which passed them by. Their minds were still thinking of how pleasant a town Tamna had been, and how they were hoping to encounter more like it on their journey.

About this they talked while they cooked the cheeses and meats that Hana's mother had prepared for them. They drank some tea after dinner, sharing a calabash cup and wooden straw, before falling into a deep sleep beneath their many layers of lamna wools. Or at least Roberto did. This night, it was Geronimo who could not find his sleep, and he awoke full of energy at half-moon, when it was at its highest point in the sky.

He rolled outside, awkwardly pulling at the blankets and sheets that covered him, since the nest of leaves had been left back in Tamna. High above where they were, at the top of the opposing canyon, Geronimo could just about make out a stone fortification, from where a faint light and shadows were dancing.

'That must be Les Orageistes!' he thought, and turned back to wake up Roberto, but, in his haste, Geronimo got caught up in the surrounding sheets, and began to roll down towards the water. As he picked up speed, Geronimo saw the tower reflected in a silver glow in the lake, with seas of stars shining in its depths. When at last he hit the water, he found that, strangely, he did not slow down. Rather, he continued moving downward, but instead of reaching the lakebed, Geronimo was now floating towards the reflection. Up to the skies Geronimo rose, despite his stomach still feeling like it was falling, till eventually he manoeuvred onto the rocky outcrop where the tower stood. This was all quite odd.

Geronimo felt like someone who had been deeply gazing at a painting, only to be awoken and find he was now inside it. He looked down towards where Roberto and the tent had been, but instead, saw nothing. Looking up to the sky where he had been falling into, he saw it was now much darker, and the moon no longer hung up above.

There were no more stars either, yet a strange white dust, cold to the touch, was now falling from the heavens. Geronimo grew worried, thinking he had knocked some of the stars as he fell, and that those same stars were now broken and falling, growing thick on the ground beneath him. The once golden flame inside the building now seemed hotter somehow, reflecting blues and silvers out through its windows.

'I hope the giants know what's going on,' said Geronimo, as he went inside.

Roberto awoke with a jolt. It was still early, or late, depending on which day you think it was, and the sun was not yet awake. All was quiet and he couldn't work out what it was exactly that made him wake so suddenly. He turned over again, but the silence was too loud to be normal, and he saw that Geronimo was no longer by him. At first, this didn't strike him as being strange, but when he saw the pile of blankets lying outside the tent, he began to worry.

There was no sign of Geronimo anywhere, but the sheets seemed to lead towards the shore, so he climbed down. In the centre of the lake, an orange glow gleamed amongst the reflection of the fading stars. It was the same light that Geronimo had seen, yet Roberto could not have known this. He waded out into the water, worried that his friend may have rolled in by accident (for Roberto was very observant, as you can see) - but saw no sign of Geronimo anywhere. Growing worried, his gaze fell back on the light on the hillside.

'If Geronimo had seen that, I'm sure he would have been attracted to it, but his lamna is still here, so he could never have got up there alone.' Then it occurred to him, that whoever was up there might well have seen what had happened, so he started to get himself ready to go up. It was not so far, perhaps a few hundred metres in altitude, but, with the help of Geronimo's lamna, he was already well on his way by the time dawn broke - though it broke softly and smoothly, like blue tea being poured over the world, and not like a dropped cup.

The mountain roads were much wider up here, and he realised he must be near to the giant's country. The last of the stars turned off their lights overhead, and the sky was bright and crisp, much like a new canvas waiting for a painter. The building he had seen from afar now grew larger, that is to say, closer, but *was* also larger than he had been expecting, when he saw it from far off.

Knocking on the big brass door handle, there was no response. A clanging of pots and pans from the other side caught his attention. He went round quietly, but not *too* quietly, as to make it seem that he was a burglar. At the rear, there was a lovely little table set for morning tea. Well, it would have been a lovely little table, if it wasn't so large.

Roberto called out to greet whoever's home he had stumbled upon, (careful not to assume too much about the inhabitants, in spite of the size of their table), only to hear a great clatter of plates fall and smash.

'*Now, look what you've done!*' screeched a deep voice from inside, '*You've broken the fee-fi-fo-fast!*'

A faint mist was now rising from the morning dew.

'Oh come on, didn'you hear that noise?' replied another voice, this one sweeter and less coarse than the first. Roberto didn't know whether to call out and say hello, or to run away, so he moved towards the gable door, where the top half was pulled back, and he waved.

This time, both of them dropped the crockery they were carrying, and Roberto wondered why they had so many dishes for the meal anyway, since there only seemed to be these two in the whole valley.

'And who might you be?' said the pair in unison, peering down at Roberto.

'I'm Roberto.' He responded, not quite sure what else to say. The pair looked at each other with equal confusion, saying 'Are we supposed to know who he is?' before carrying on doing what they were doing, taking no further notice of him.

'Are you the giants?' he asked eventually, thinking that they weren't as big as he had expected. Larger than average, certainly, but not as big as the roads would make them seem. In fact the shorter one would really be considered quite short, if they weren't so tall. The first was stout and round, with the beginnings of a little moustache sprouting above their lip. The other looked younger, with rosy cheeks and a more inviting smile. The first only grimaced painfully for a moment as they greeted Roberto. This shorter giant seemed to take offence at being called a giant, and corrected Roberto by saying, 'We are Les Orageistes, or; The Storm-Bringers, as you might call us in the little-people speak.'

This clumsy pair, in matching orange dungarees and green hats, did not look much like 'storm-bringers' – they could possibly rustle up a cold spell, or a rainy day at worst, but of course Roberto didn't tell *them* that. It was rather hard for him to pronounce 'Lay Zoraj Easts' as it sounded to him, so he asked what each of their names were.

'Bidon was my first name.' Said the shorter.
'Byron.' Said the taller.

These were much easier to say.
They then invited the unexpected guest to dine.
That is to say.
To breakfast with them, albeit somewhat cold-heartedly compared to Tamna.

The spread comprised of cold hams and pale cheeses, and
The tea was rather brown and tasteless.

The cutlery was also embarrassingly large, even for the giants, which
made the pair look far too small to be real giants. At length, Roberto got up
the courage to ask them if they had perhaps seen a little green egg person
throughout the night.

'Why do people always come to *us!* to solve their problems? Every
traveller makes the echtra up to us, then asks us for advice? How would living
up here, away from everything and everyone *possibly* make us somehow
sapient?' This outburst from Bidon surprised even Byron, who said softly,
'Oh please excuse Bidon, they haven't quite fallen awake yet, and this tea isn't
terribly decaffeinated. You see, we often guest many receivers like you, who
are similarly answering some looks, and we often help to try them, but
without any luck.'

'Quit muddling your words Byron,' said Bidon sharply from behind
the bucket of tea they were holding, before turning back to Roberto.

'Look kid, whatever jewel you're looking for, whatever princess
needs saving, whatever weapon you seek, we aren't the ones to tell you where
it is. Some storyteller out there keeps telling kids that Giants on mountains
always know what to do, or where to go, so they send them up the hill to us,
as if being *larger* than average makes us wiser.' Bidon lingered on the word
"larrrger" longer than was needed, reminding Roberto how small they were
for giants.

'But I'm not looking for any of those, my friend seems to have
wandered from our camp down there throughout the night, and I can't find
him anywhere.' This response surprised the pair, and their eyes opened
slightly.

'Well now, that is hearing to interest!' said Byron, and Roberto wasn't really sure what way those bees were supposed to word. The pair of giants looked at each other and shrugged.

'Alright then, listen up,' said Bidon. 'Think of a door.'
'And what do you see?' Byron continued.
'A brown piece of wood?'
'And a hole for a key?'
'But the most important question…'
'That you should think upon…'
'Is - is that door open?'
'And what do you see?'

Roberto closed his eyes and thought. He remembered how he had emerged from the chaos, walking onto the beach, to find Geronimo. His memories lacked colour, and everything was tinted shades of silver. A sweet, gentle voice, deep within his mind spoke to him.

'Mountains of clouds, skies of seas, isles of stars, rocks like rains, clouds of mountains, skies of rocks, rains like stars…..' on and on it went until he was dreamily falling into a trance.

'Oi!' shouted Bidon from across the table.

'Think of a deer, and what do you see?' Byron said dreamily, to precisely no-one in particular, 'Is he dancing beneath deep-elm tree?'

'Oi!' said Bidon again. Roberto jumped back into reality. Byron had wandered off inside, coming back shortly after with an accordion strapped to their chest.

'Is he caged up, is he carved up?' sang Byron in a melancholic tone. 'On broke bended knee?'

Bidon was contemptuously glaring at Byron. 'Cut that out!' they shouted.

Roberto's thoughts were elsewhere, and centred on that serow on Mt. Bokoro.

'Geronimo must have went into a cave!' he exclaimed internally.

'Worked it all out, have ya?' said Bidon, 'Yeah, riddles often make it easier to think unclearly. Only then is it simple to see straight.' 'Simple to see straight,' repeated Byron.

Roberto felt only in his gut that he was right, but oftentimes it's your gut alone that makes your decisions.

'Is there a cave on this mountain?' he asked, rather abruptly considering the circumstances (the circumstances having been quite quiet up until now).

'Why yes, just on the other side, but there's been some strange folk nearby it lately.' Byron replied. 'You could make it there by this afternoon, just follow the Pontyz Pass. We'll be going along it for a spell, on our way up to the peak, but we can go together until the junction.'

Roberto agreed to this plan, and they finished up a dessert of some cake called 'Flan-Flan' – pronounced 'Flawng-Flawng' in their funny accents, before an argument ensued about who had eaten all the flan-flan.

> 'Ew ey leu flawng-flawng?'
> 'Say lah leu flawng-flawng!'
> 'Say too leu flawng flawng?'
> 'Weee! Say tout le flan-flan!'

They bickered on like this for a while, and it became almost time for the second meal of the still young day - though they agreed to skip this, as there weren't enough clouds in the sky, and someone might grow suspicious

that Les Orageistes were not doing their work. And so, they went inside to
gather up their bags of instruments, which they explained were used to play
the weather. Their kites too, which they used to guide the winds, and they set
off. The day was so calm that Roberto thought there was no chance of their
kites being able to fly, but they threw them up so high, and with such force,
that they managed to catch some hidden river of wind away off in the
heavens, and dragged them behind themselves to give their sails an extra push
(or rather, a pull).

They walked together along the narrow mountain road – the Pontyz
Pass - which Roberto supposed was named for the 'Pointies' – the word the
giants used for the sharp, jagged rocks which poked out from the ground. The
path turned sharply upwards towards the Zapateca mountain, where Les
Orageistes explained they would part ways, and Roberto should continue
straight around the side, along the 'little people road' to get to the ruined cave

'We are in a good mood today, so you should be fine on that
narrower stretch - in the rains it's pretty treacherous.' Bidon told him, though
what Roberto considered a mild to moderate mood must have been good by
their standards.

As they walked away uphill, Roberto could hear Byron's accordion
softly playing in the distance, but it seemed somehow to get louder, as they
got further away, before being accompanied by Bidon's great drum, before
both faded slowly away together into the distant ambience of morning. When
finally, they had drifted into echoes, Roberto became acutely aware of how
alone he was, (Lamnas don't make for very good conversationalists) and soon
his thoughts bounced rapidly between flowing waters, damp caves, rocks of
rains, mountains of clouds…

Time passes very differently when you are on your own. Moments in
your memories can be hours, and minutes on clocks can become millennia in
your mind. The only thing that kept him on track were the steady beats of his

footsteps sounding loudly throughout the canyon. Even these, doof-doofing along, without any winds to disturb their vibrations, bounced endlessly on the rocks before falling back up to Roberto's ears. Then there was the lamna's clumsy clippity-cloppity-clip-clop, which sounded like an accountant trying to play maraccas.

Doof-doof-clippity-cloppity-doof-doof-clip-clop-doof-doof-clippity... they went on and on for some time. Some time that is, for it was almost impossible to tell how much time it actually was. Somewhere amongst all this, Roberto heard another noise, a clickety sort of a noise, a clickety-clackity, from some high-up bird. He squinted as it flew, for he had not brought his trusty binoculars with him, but Roberto was sure it was Albert, even if he seemed to take no notice of his admirer (probably searching for some bugs, thought Roberto). The bird flew over a neighbouring mountaintop with ease, and swooped down to some unseen low point in the next valley.

So distracted was Roberto by all this, as they rounded the pass to the mountain's northern side, that he didn't even notice a great pair of wings swoop down behind him, until it said, 'Careful now.' It was Alfred.

Roberto didn't quite know what to say, so Alfred said it for him.

'I see you've lost your friend.'

Roberto nodded.

'What makes you think he's over there?' Alfred asked.

Roberto felt a bit silly, saying that it was his gut, but at this, Alfred only smiled slightly, as much as a bird with a beak can, and said, 'Well, as long as you didn't think logically, then I'm sure you're right.'

VI
Ejército Zapotec

On a sudden, many things happened at once.

First, a raincloud burst open like a balloon on the jagged cliff face above. Then, Roberto fumbled and fell, as the ground below him broke away. He rolled as rocks fell on top, and beneath him, before finally coming to a halt in some sort of a hollow cavern. There were leafy shrubs and dank mosses all around, which had broken his fall, and the lamna beside was stunned, but all things considered, they were in good shape.

Light peered in from holes above, and sandy stones poked out beside a path which led further downwards. Alfred had seemed to vanish as soon as he had appeared, that is, if he was ever there at all, and there was no easy way back up to where the path had given way, so, after dusting himself off, and checking that the lamna could stand, they began to walk deeper into the damp depths below.

Rains crept through the rocks and slid down the smooth walls, revealing carvings within the powdery sides. They showed strange insects, with horns like rhinoceroses, fat fishes floating over towns of people, and sparks of lightning attacking large triangular buildings.

The pictures seemed to tell a story, though not a very happy one. Roberto supposed (again, quite correctly) that these markings had been made by the same people shown there, who had probably come here underground long ago to escape the great calamity depicted on the wall. His mind was not left to linger long upon these images, for he heard voices coming from further along the path. He could not understand all that they were saying, but now and again they would say some words he recognised from Pashtamna, though their voices were much harsher, and they made a phlegmy sort of noise at the back of their throat when they said a 'h'.

Now, Roberto was certainly a friendly fellow, who always said hello to most everyone he met, but if you were in his position, alone and facing two strangers in a darkened place, you too would have done as he did, which was to jump and hide beneath a pile of rocks, just away from where he had fallen. He was worried that the lamna, in its simple animalistic way, might give up the game, but animals are often much smarter than people when they sense danger, which is why it's almost impossible to catch a wild bird with your hands. Go on. Try it.

The voices grew louder, and light danced on the cavern's walls. Their equipment and armour looked much like Garuda's, except newer and shinier, with pistolettes on their waists, and torches which were not orange and warm like a cosy fireplace. No, these torches were burning blue-silvery hot, and reminded Roberto of the Bunsen burners he had seen in his chemistry classes at school. He assumed they must also be burning Bunsen, in order to glow that colour. The bright light was so close to the guards' faces that thankfully they didn't notice Roberto, which pretty much defeated the purpose of having such a bright torch, but of course Roberto wasn't going to tell *them* that.

They passed by, completely unawares, before grumpily going over to the newly formed pile of rocks, and marking on a sheet of paper the cause of the disturbance. This task took them a good deal of time (however long that is), as they were obliged to tick many boxes, sign their names (several times) and use a variety of multicoloured stamps to make their work official. When they were done, and had lazily checked to see no signs of life, the pair trodded back along the path they had come from.

After they had moved away, just out of earshot, eyeshot, and presumably gunshot, Roberto motioned to the lamna to move quietly, and they followed the guards. The lamna, for all its clumsiness earlier, appeared to understand the situation, and managed to tread only on the softest ground, which resulted in a sort of cli, clo, cli, clo, noise, which blended rather well with the pitter-patter of the raindrops.

Roberto was now, arguably, the louder of the pair, for his bags were making an awful shuffling sort of racket, even if he hadn't packed his tennis gear. Despite this, the guards were now far enough away that they couldn't hear their rattle, and talked so loudly and continuously that it would be unlikely they would hear anything besides each other anyway.

The wide tunnels wound and twisted past more gaps where the land above had subsided, allowing the intricate patterns and designs to be easily seen - glinting gold and silver in the trickling sunlight. After a few minutes, they could hear many more voices, and the tunnel opened into a large hall with many guards tending to their camp. Flags on the walls said 'Ejército Zapotec' and there seemed to be a small city set up within this great hollow hillside. Rewinding the steps he had taken to get here, Roberto supposed that this must have been where he had seen Albert descend into the valley.

The columns of smoke from the cookhouses were just about the only sign that could give the camp's location away, though the space was so tall that the thick brown clouds had dispersed into wisps by the time they reached the open air above. Roberto wisely kept his distance from all the comings and goings on, perched behind a cluster of high rocks. Surveying the area (and once again wishing he had brought his binoculars), he could see a narrow stream running through the room, lots of pickaxes and machinery, men with wide brimmed hats, gamnas with wide hooves, and nestled right in the centre, was a long sandy tent, much bigger than the rest, which was evidently the quarters of General Santos.

Roberto shuddered at the thought of entering such a hostile-looking encampment, all greys and drab shades of beige, full of thick smog and clanging tools, guarded by very tall, very strong men. Something then rustled behind him, and Roberto turned to see the sleek rounded face of a slender black dog. At first, he was frightened, assuming the dark beast belonged to the men, and would bark to alert them, but this never happened. Its gaze merely lingered softly on him for a moment, before it turned away and lightly bounded off through the rubble around the camp's perimeter.

Roberto paused for a moment, unsure whether to follow it or not. Despite its sombre, menacing appearance, there was a tender sadness dwelling deep within those eyes, and his gut, which had guided him thus far, told him to go. He took off his bags, laying them beside the lamna, before patting it firmly on the head to indicate it to stay put, and quickly took off behind the dog. The lamna did as it was told, or was implied, and set its head down to hide, but also to have a short doze. Roberto ducked and dived as gently as he could, for the dog was now well ahead, though it seemed to be waiting for him just at the edge of his sight.

The pass was very well hidden, in fact Roberto was sure he would never have been able to follow it without the dog's guidance. It wove into the walls, through cracks no thicker than Roberto's stomach, and down holes which seemed only to be big enough for rabbits, but were (thankfully) much larger inside. In this way, he eventually reached what he supposed to be the northern end of the encampment – but the black dog had disappeared.

Peering out from one of the holes, it seemed a reasonably short skirmish from where he was, up to the tent, where he hoped to lift back an awning and slip inside unnoticed. He awaited for the coast to be clear, and made a dash across to the opposite side of the road. Down a narrow alley and up a short hill, he made it, pulled the peg, and peeled back the corner of the tent. Luckily, he seemed to have entered into some kind of a store-house, for there were barrels of wines, crates of chests, and coffers of copper all around.

Roberto took a moment to breathe, before continuing to look around. The whole tent seemed to be made up of one large roof, with great wooden cargo boxes (about three cubic metres each) separating the space into rooms, just like the partitions at Hana's house.

This suited Roberto very well, since it meant he was able to easily slip up into the space between the blocks and the rafters, moving freely between the chambers. All the guards wore such sturdy, heavy helmets that very few of them ever took the time to look up – it was easier to stare at their feet.

This headquarters contained a small town contained within the small city contained within the cavern, with every partitioned space serving a different function. In the different rooms he saw, in no particular order; a buzz-saw, a carpenter's workshop, a dental chair, an elephant, a fuse box, a great statue, a harp, an interrogation chamber, and GERONIMO! Thankfully not being interrogated.

No, Geronimo was sitting up cosy in the main hall, where excavations were taking place. He looked almost like junior royalty there, for he had now some sort of liquid metal ball to move about upon. The brass sphere he rested on must have felt like a cushion, after spending days in the forest rolling about on those spiky twigs and sharp leaves. Geronimo hadn't seen Roberto yet, still being well occupied with his work, which seemed to be managing a group of archaeologists who were unearthing a small part of some large dusty fountain. Beside Geronimo stood a tall man with a sandy-coloured cap and a thick dark beard.

Well, at first he seemed tall, till Roberto saw he was clumsily marching around on a pair of very thick-soled boots, and his opaque black sunglasses made him look so much more strong and powerful than he probably was. This was undoubtedly the infamous General Santos. Roberto recognised him vaguely from some far-off distant memory, but he couldn't quite place it.

The pair were inspecting the half-covered fountain where its silvery waters shone brightly against the white torches. Geronimo seemed to be doing most of the talking, while the General was deep in his beard, stroking his thoughts and nodding along with whatever Geronimo was telling him. Roberto shuffled over to the most lefternmost side of the chamber that he could get to, and he was just about able to make out some of the conversation, which went as follows:

Geronimo: 'If I've told you it once, I've told you a thousand times, I
              was by the lake, I stumbled and fell into the reflection, and
              then someone pulled me out from this water!'

Santos: 'Hmmm…'

Geronimo: 'I suppose the moon was bright that night, but I'm not
              even sure anymore, since you keep asking "And how bright
              was the moon? What were its phases? Did the phase have a
              nose?'

Santos: 'Hmmm?'

Geronimo: 'I said, I mightn't have noticed how bright the moon was,
              it's normally about the same.'

Santos: 'No, the nose part.'

Geronimo:	'What nose?'
Santos:	'The moon's nose.'
Geronimo:	'Yes, it might snow on the moon, but who knows?'
Santos:	'No, the moon's nose, you know…'
Geronimo:	'Oh, that nose! No, I don't know.'
Santos:	'Hmmm…'

And so, they rambled on.

The General remained surprisingly patient for a man of his menacing demeanour, but seemed to be slowly easing out the full story from Geronimo, who was evidently enjoying the bouncy flow of the words themselves more than his counterpart. From what he could make out, Roberto guessed Geronimo had not got here too long before him, and was not in any immediate danger, so he remained quiet and observant from his lofty nest.

The fountain was still running, with a smaller upper tier dripping down into a much bigger basin below. Parts of it were still being carved out from the bedrock, but he could just about make out the word 'Veritas' on the higher bowl, and 'Áthas' on the lower pool. Roberto thought there must be a lot of sand or dust in the higher one, as its waters seemed a lot duller and yellower than the dark cool gleam coming from below.

When he moved, he could see that the fountain depicted two ladies standing one on top of the other. A round, jovial face marked the side of the bottom jug, while the toppermost had a sadder expression, albeit with a stronger and more focused gaze, which reminded him of Hana.

Though much of the workers' attentions were directed upon the bottom basin (as that was evidently where Geronimo had arrived from), Roberto found himself transfixed by the unhappy smile of Veritas.

The general was pacing back and forth, coaxing all the information he could from Geronimo, who happily talked away without ever seeming to put much thought into what he was saying. In spite of the oppressive atmosphere, there was no obvious reason for Roberto to be afraid of the General and his Men. Yet, to any outsider looking at the situation, and from the alcove he had made his way in to, it would certainly seem like it was Roberto, who was the threat! This left him with a conundrum to pickle. He could reveal himself now, and hope Geronimo would speak quickly in support of him (though in so doing he would more likely risk immediate capture) or, to wait until there were fewer guards, and perhaps an opening would appear wherein to reveal himself.

Despite the former plan appealing to his senses - being a young boy and still brash in his decision-making - he had never met any nice people who kept interrogation chambers in their houses and that encouraged him to wait for another moment. It was just as well that he did so, for otherwise, he would not have gleaned a valuable morsel of information.

Eventually, Santos grew weary of hearing Geronimo telling, then re-telling the account of how he had arrived through the fountain, and ordered that a room be made up for his new guest. Around half of the dozen or so workers there went off to build a partition for Geronimo, but Roberto felt his friend would be safe enough with them. He continued watching the General, who now took a metal case from his breast-pocket, opened it, took out a long black stick of what seemed to be incense, put it into his mouth, and set fire to it.

Why on earth he did such a thing was unclear, for he spent the next half-minute coughing and going rather pale. After waving it around the room for another thirty seconds or so, he smelt it one last time, before throwing it as hard as he could against the ground, where it sparked with a great blue flash.

His coughing had now developed into something more in line with a dry heave, 'Broo-ha, broooo-haha broouu-hah' he choked out, while the workers continued as normal, as if nothing was wrong. Then a most peculiar thing happened. The smoke which rose from where the stick had been extinguished now seemed to be congealing and shifting into an amorphous blob. Then, the edges wore off, and the clear outline of a skull remained, glaring towards the General.

'Belén! Oh how good it is to see you!' Santos sounded quite nervous as he said this.

'What is it.' The skull responded abruptly, not even taking the time to add the appropriate punctuation.

'Well, errr, your majesty, err, we have uncovered something quite, errr, interrr-esting today - a fountain.' Santos seemed quite pathetic now beside this skull, which now turned to look at the fountain. As it is impossible for a skull to show an emotion, it decided that the next best step was to spit a flame at the top of the fountain, though the clay was only slightly scorched.

'Ughhh!' it screeched (which was unlikely the response that Santos was expecting) before continuing, 'Destroy this ugly statue growing on top! I'm sick of my dirty sister working her way into everything I do. Long ago, this is what the people called me, Áthas, but I never did like such a cheerful name. And Veritas! What a silly thing to be named! Though Hélène isn't much better... Enough! Next time you call upon me, it better be to show me what a good job you've done destroying that statue. And what of my throne? Have you polished it yet?'

'Well, err, about that, we've managed about half of it now, but a lot of the rust remains...'

'Useless fool!' and its colours swayed and drifted between grey and blue, before swirling up and passing through the roof. Though the shape seemed far off, Roberto felt it pull at him as it passed, and was sure he heard it whisper to him the words 'I know who you are' - though what *that* could mean, he did not know.

Roberto thought this as good a time as any to take his leave, and find Geronimo, for the General stood afterwards in a brief embarrassed daze, and the workers had set down their tools in the astonishment of seeing their leader spoken to in such a diminishing fashion.

Roberto scurried along the beam, crossing into an adjoining partition, where guards were busily building crates and separating a block for Geronimo, who was himself happily distracting them from their work, asking them questions like 'Where do you come from? 'Do you speak Pashtmna?' and 'What time is it?'

To which they replied, 'Cities.' 'Almost.' 'Breaktime.' And at that, they all sat down and took out little lunch boxes of square sandwiches with wide bread much like the loaves in Tamna Town. Geronimo too, strangely started to nibble on his brass cushion, and bit a bit off! Much like a blob of jelly though, it began to grow back almost as soon as he had swallowed it - it probably felt as therapeutic as trimming one's nails, or picking a scab.

Amongst all this crunching and gobbling, Roberto figured that no-one would notice the sound of him snacking on the bright red grupelberry he had tucked into his pocket earlier, so he kicked back, crossed his legs and gazed upwards at the rafters as he ate it. He was, it seems, much too relaxed, for he carelessly tossed its core down to his right, right onto a guard's head, just as casually as if he had been sitting in a field.

The guard's reaction was... quick enough, though at first they had all jumped away from it, thinking it was some sort of explosive. Naturally, as all good soldiers do, they drew their scimitar blades to combat it, before instead reaching for their wooden shields too, to protect them from the oncoming blast.

By the time they thought to look up, Roberto was already down beside them, at Geronimo's side, and STILL none of them really noticed him. They were instead clunkily dropping their swords and shields to pull out the rifles on their backs, as they began searching the ceiling for the source of the hoax. This gave Roberto & Geronimo time to catch up, exchanging pleasantries, birthday cards, dinner invitations, and such like, etc. &c. so forth and so on, *ad nauseum.*

Seeing the boy so naturally acquainted with this strange egg, the soldiers dropped their guard, and started asking him questions such as 'You bomba maké?' 'Ghoou kyu?' though not in quite as primitive a manner as it may look on paper. They were friendly enough, patiently waiting for Roberto to come up with some basic Pashtamna answers for them, with Geronimo helping to translate, as and when required. Another man amongst the guards was now translating into another tongue, shouting aloud to his comrades in a deep bellowing voice. They all shouted strange words to each other, like "ohmbudsmanzinkwaiiuree" and "independentachoodictation" before the collective opinion was translated first into Pashtamna, explained to Geronimo, then translated once more for Roberto.

So frankly, nothing made very much sense throughout the ensuing first few minutes of conversation. That is, until they could finally agree on one, easy way to translate the term "nothing" into each other's tongue. And so, they settled on doing nothing to this new intruder, carrying on with their afternoon's work as usual, as if nothing had happened at all. And, in the end, as they had formally agreed upon it, 'nothing' truly happened.

Nothing then happened, until the General himself came to check up on his guest, and subsequently flew into a rage that none of his troops had alerted him to the presence of another outsider. He shouted at the whole regiment individually and managed to find a valid reason to chastise every single one of them equally.

For you see, the reason behind this mishap, as the pair would later find out from the General himself, was due to a very fair quirk within General Santos' ranks. Each guard was treated in the same way, as he had dissolved all formal hierarchy and titles, encouraging his men to "manage themselves and their neighbour," which he had discovered would noticeably improve their morale.

Later, when he was calmer than at present, they found Santos to be a very pleasant man, a talented conversationalist, fluent in several languages, and terribly witty, though Roberto always thought it strange, how he was the only one who had not relinquished his title of 'General.'

When at last he had finished with his scoldings, he turned to Roberto & Geronimo, who, in the meantime, had been filling each other in on what they had been up to whilst apart. It seemed Geronimo had fallen into some sort of a dreamworld when he hit the water, and his mind had shown him bits of memories, only they were "all jumbled up y'know!"

This had very much excited Geronimo, but when he was pulled out by one of the guards, he found himself covered in this coating of bronze liquid, much like how you might feel when you step into a pile of cool seaweed on a hot summer's day at the beach. Not unpleasant, but at the same time, not something you want hanging around your toes. Geronimo had tried to shake it off, and it dripped down to the floor, where he found it made his most comfortable cushion so far. He called it his "aretē" and was certain it had been comprised of all those jumbled memories that flew past him underwater. It could well have been, for it shone with a dull, majestic glow,

like an ancient king's broadsword that is only beginning to rust after two
thousand years.

Whatever metal it was, it was magnificent to see such a clean shine
of copper beside Geronimo's green face, and the colours complimented each
other cordially. Accordingly, the simple fact that it looked metallic, was
enough for these soldiers of the 'Ejército Zapotec' – or, the 'Zapatistas' for
short, to be convinced that Geronimo was very valuable, which in turn
explained why Geronimo was not quite considered a prisoner, and more like a
treasure.

You see, by the by-laws in their land, this was enough to disqualify
Geronimo's entrapment as a standard prisoner of war. Though where exactly
Roberto fit in, charged with being an accessory to a treasure, was not clear, as
no-one could agree upon one single regulation upon which to legally charge
him. And so, in the end, after much further deliberation, nothing happened.

Roberto & Geronimo were at least granted free roam of the camp,
which included, (owing to the generosity of Santos) free health care,
complimentary food and drink vouchers, and a taxi transport service.

Under the General's orders, the Ejército were required to maintain a
fleet of small pick-up trucks and jeeps in continuous transit around the camp.
The troops were permitted to jump onboard any which one which was going
in whichever direction they needed. They travelled only in straight lines,
meaning the soldiers would jump off at crossroads to continue their journeys
on the back of the next passing vehicle, as all the roads were sensibly
organised into neat little squares.

This was all very efficient, and allowed the pair to spend the evening
touring the many different archaeological digs taking place in the camp.
Though not before they had gracefully accepted invitations to sup with the
General in his quarters that night around nine. The builders were finishing
their work around five, and around the same time Roberto & Geronimo

stepped outside the tent and out into the softer evening light. They had spent the afternoon there, fooling around with the instruments and trinkets the General had removed from the ruins.

The streets seemed quieter now, and the heavy-thick air was thinner, since most of the workers had already gone back to their barracks for their evening meal. Roberto & Geronimo simply took a rounded flatbread from a lady grilling them on one of the street corners. She also offered them a small topping of red tapenade with it, which of course they gladly accepted.

As they walked, Roberto told Geronimo of his meeting with the Orageistes, whilst also learning from Geronimo of some of the reasonings behind Santos' 'ejército' - which was the city's word for something between an exercise, an excursion, and an extraction of precious metals - though Santos had no interest in mining ores.

No, his interest lay only with metal objects, crafted and created by ancient peoples, hidden deep within the mountains. Santos did not particularl enjoy discovering a lump of copper filled with stones and sand, but instead he could think of many uses for a cup, or a knife, made many moons before by a skilled hand. This was easily seen in the piles of bronze which sat beside each dig station. Where Roberto was from, these were very valuable, very useful ingredients to make all sorts of tools and equipment – there were even big nuggets of gold just poking out from walls, though no-one seemed to pay them any attention.

Instead, they focused their attentions on the shiny silver treasures which were dotted about the place. These seemed to hold some special significance for Santos, who had hoarded much of them within his own tent. The workers were left with what elsewhere would be considered the prime booty, the golden cutlery and crockery. They clumsily clanked them together at the little bars set up at the roadside, where they sat on short stools and had loud conversations with their neighbours. The pair went up to one, where there sat an old man with blackened teeth and a cracked smile, and asked him what exactly this concoction, a pale, bitter-smelling drink was, and why every person around seemed to be drinking it.

He told them (after some rough translating) that it was a sort of a juice, made from a fermented 'Ha-Ná' flower. He explained how this flower is only found deep in the forests, and is white with pink edges. It has a very strong scent, almost like a fragrant incense, and men from the city often drink it a lot, to remember the happier times when they were younger and had time to play out in the woods. They also played cards there at the table, each one decorated in differing numbers of flowers, denoting their perceived worth, or value, within the contexts of the games.

The evening progressed relentlessly, and Roberto & Geronimo felt they should get ready to sup with the General and his cabinet. It was to be a rather proper sort of affair, and neck ties and collars were required. They went to a hastily-built tailors, where old ladies spun them around and sewed them just as quickly as they could, to produce handsome formal suits in under a quarter of an hour.

Thumbing their way back, on the back of passing trucks, the pair were ready just in time for the entrées, consisting of layered plates of sandwiches, biscuits, and other appetite-whetters, being delivered round the main antechamber to all the General's most elite companions and distinguished guests. They had all agreed upon a communal evening repas to convene on the exciting discovery of Geronimo.

The bustling hall grew silent as the pair rolled and walked in respectively, and respectfully. A stunned shock pervaded the room, the officers stood to attention, before collectively applauding the General for his discovery - even though none of the archaeologists they had seen earlier were present. Only groups of tall and taller men, who showed little emotion from behind their clear eyeglasses and colourful shawls which hid half of their faces. General Santos stood, resplendent in his suit, and greeted both, as his guests of honour.

They mingled for five minutes or so, then proceeded swiftly through the grand old archway, into the dining hall, where seats were set for twenty-three high-ranking officials, such as members of their parliament, admiralty, vice-admiralty, royalty (defunct), pharmaceutical firms, bankers, gold-diggers and grave-diggers (The latter finding themselves there through no more trait of their own, other than their throughotherness).

Roberto & Geronimo held back slightly, to let the others take their places, organising themselves into rank and importance. Santos came along and shuffled them forward with him, up, up to the head of the table, to sit with him at his right-hand side.

Some doctors of an unclear discipline had weaved their way up to the highest-ranking seats on the other side of the table, peering excitedly across, nudging their neighbour at the sight of Geronimo.

The discovery of whatever metal was attached to Geronimo was obviously of the utmost interest to their studies, for they were hurriedly jotting down notes on a pair of small block pocketbooks.

It later turned out that this copper alloy-like material was almost identical to the bronze coating which had grown like a mould over the throne they had been set to work on restoring, though the key difference seemed to lie in the vast quantities of trace elements, observed within Geronimo's ball. Of these, the scientists had already succeeded in isolating particles of wood, soil, sand, air, rivers, coconuts, and a sticky substance which appeared to pull all of it together.

Deeming it 'worthy of further chemical and academical research' they judged that it, and its creator, Geronimo, should be brought back to the Mino Tower in Ballyna, where it would be assessed by both the Astrognomers and the Falconers.

These peoples would work together to cross-examine the new discoveries using an experiment called 'The Process' whereby the subjects would be investigated scientifically over the course of several weeks.

The table consisted mostly of these two groups of people, with some others of Tamna or Ballyna descent, all in charge of the management of the excavations of the 'Ejército Zapotec.'

To the left of Roberto sat a quiet Falconer, who did not speak much throughout the evening. He was chief of the Falconers for this gathering - for they hold amongst themselves a simple ritual to decide the pecking order, when a group of them convenes together. The younger sit only on the right-hand side of the elder, and this one was the oldest, though he looked only around fifty years of age.

His name was Captain Clint Lewis Caribou, and he spoke with a voice both soft and strong, gentle in his annunciation of words, with exotic trills and motifs trailing from his tongue - that is, when he spoke at all. The others in the room were all speaking in hurried, excited tones, quickly changing languages, almost to the point of showing off. But the group of hooded men sat quietly, whispering information to their neighbour while listening closely to the conversations of their counterparts on the opposite side of the table.

Roberto was having trouble understanding the meaning of all the words being said, though some parts made sense, if he listened acutely. The consensus at the end of the discussions was as follows: first, they were to eat. Then, they were to drink. Then they would speak some more, eat some more, and then drink some more. Finally, they would sleep. After they had done this, the plan for tomorrow would be drawn up.

It was scheduled to consist of arranging a convoy of trucks to bring the newfound treasures down the mountain to the Somato train line, from whence they would be conveyed to the capital, Ballyna, for further investigation.

It had been a long time since Roberto last travelled by train, so he was rather excited by this plan - though he couldn't shake off the feeling that they were being taken along as a kind of liberal prisoner, rather than as thanks to some act of kindness.

END OF VOLUME TWO

...mountains of clouds,

...skies of seas,

...isles of stars,

...rains of rocks

VOLUME THREE

VII
Ballyna

VIII
Providencia

IX
Samsara

PARTIE FINALE

VII
Ballyna

Ejército Express, Morning Edition – *The camp was awoken late last night by a commotion caused by a rogue lamna. The suspect was apprehended at the scene. Officers have already marked it for removal by means of expulsion.*

The next morning, the camp awoke much earlier than their superior officers, with the bosses rolling out of their hammocks around three working hours after the diggers and drivers had already taken up their tools. Deep work songs resonated from those caverns dug into the mountainside; thick pulsating chants all made in time with the clinks of metal pickaxes on hollow sandy walls.

Provisions had been set aside for the outbound trucks; their drivers dusting down upholstery for the dignified, though tardy, elites. Roberto & Geronimo rolled out in about an hour's advance on this group; setting themselves up early in the dining hall and making the most of the royal spread being served there for breakfast. Fine cheeses, cuts of meats, breads and cups of tea and coffee, over which they discussed what might await them in the city. The idea of being couped up, picked on and examined for many weeks on end was not appealing to either of them, and they hoped The Process would be over as quickly as possible.

In a sense, it was. Everything began to pass them by very quickly, with many trivial things happening continuously. All of these kept them highly occupied; allowing time to pass freely by. Despite the late awakening group of commanders, the breakfast platters were quickly gobbled up, and the officers had their morning 'toilet'. This was how they described 'getting ready for work' in their language, and I'll have you know it means the exact same thing in your language - so stop sniggering!

The guards loaded the last treasures onto the trucks, weighing them to ensure they aren't too 'lourd' (or heavy, as we might say, though personally, I think 'lourd' is a much heavier-sounding word) before finally balancing each pair of wheels to ensure stability. The company loaded in, with much of the same crowd as the previous evening, arranging themselves similarly to how they did at the dinner table, Roberto & Geronimo at the back of the same truck.

Again, Captain Clint was beside Roberto, and seemed to be in a chirpier mood today. He told the pair many tales about his previous life back in the city, hundreds of years ago when he was a young man. He rhymed off lists of peoples who lived there, the women, the men, the reds, the lefts, the Greeks and the blues; to name just a few, but they were so numerous it was hard to remember them all.

Captain Clint quickly realised that to learn so many different languages or catalogue each of the cultures distinctly would be IMPOSSIBLE in the few hours ride that they had from the Ejército to the city, simply finishing by telling the pair, 'You will see them all when you get there!'

The journey by truck was even less eventful than the walk from Tamna, as all motorised journeys are. Since the only view they had was through the opened back portion of the truck, they could only see where they had already been, and not what was coming. As luck would have it however, they could hear mechanical whirrs and buzzes coming from up ahead; as both the machinery and infrastructure grew, as they came closer to the Somato Train Line.

Industry had brought with it a lingering electrical drone, lying low within the approaching soundscape. Fruit trees were being plucked with robotic arms, clumsily breaking away branches as they went. The afternoon's gentle lull was sporadically broken by a sharp whistle or bell, or both in quick succession.

When they got out of the truck at Somato Station, they were briefly blinded by the sun's bright, reflecting off the many stalls adorned with diagonal and stepped patterns. Each of these were made in the same reds and greens and oranges and blues sewn into the patchwork clothing which the old ladies were steadily knitting.

Outside, the sounds of metal clanging on metal rang louder, no longer softened by the hum of the truck's large engine, and the sun hung hot in the heavens. The whole scene hit Roberto's senses in such a loud fashion, that he felt blinded for an instant, much like you might feel when you turn on the kitchen light late at night. Shuffling forward towards the platforms, they began to recognise there was a much more diverse group of people here – which, according to Capt. Clint, was just a taster of what Ballyna would be like.

Many similar trucks were arriving from the other dig sites, offloading their cargoes into the freight trains fastened to the back of the long carriages designed for passengers. A grand old steam engine took up the fore, its slick pistons hanging outside the wheels, a small stack of smoke arising from its spout as it stood impatiently waiting to set off along the track. The railway workers were much less interested in Geronimo than General Santos had anticipated, and steadfastly refused to offer the group upgraded tickets - in spite of their high opinion of themselves. It would still be some time until the train's departure, so the group remained outside on the platform.

The General took out a packet of breadsticks from his top-right pocket, and distributed one to each of his men, who crunched them quickly. Santos, however, held it to his lips, and sucked on it gently, much as he had done with the incense earlier. He occasionally nibbled a bit to chew on, but this would dissolve away pretty quickly. Something was clearly on his mind. His face lay vacant of expression, staring into space, and talking only rarely.

'I see you are also a foreigner in this land,' he said suddenly to Roberto, who turned to see Santos' eye fixed upon him. 'Skin so pale and hair so fair, it's a wonder that no-one else has pointed it out to you,' he continued slowly, removing the breadstick from his mouth with his fist, holding it snugly between his index and middle fingers. 'Why care ye for these island-folk? With faces dark and thick black hair?'

His voice seemed to be coming from some far-off place, and the look in his eye extended deeper into his skull than it ever possibly could. Suddenly, the trance was broken as quickly as it had begun, and Roberto was unsure if it had happened at all.

None of the other officers appeared to hear it, for they would surely have noticed such a strange tongue being spoken at their table - and Geronimo was distracted by the arrival of his lamna, with all its pouches intact. For some reason, the officers had thought its pouches were a part of some new breed of robotic lamna, and they had foregone searching inside to discover where the clinking metal noises were originating from. This arrival distracted everyone for a moment, and only Roberto remembered these cutting words from Santos, who seemed, frankly, as if he might not have heard the words himself.

Presently, whistles were blown from the train driver's cab, indicating an imminent departure; creating a new wave of furore in the station. The officers rose late and seated themselves in the front carriage. For such a long, sprawling industrial zone as Somato Station was, almost everything; the cranes, the trucks, the signs, all of it was taken away with the departing convoy, leaving almost no trace of where the station had been bustling just a few moments beforehand.

Shunting off with a slow heave, and groaning under the thousands of pounds of metals loaded upon its back, the train set off along its long straight track through the flat desert. Beyond the horizon it went, stretching to the distant edge of San Salvador, where the island met the sea once more.

Though the ground was flat, the land was at a very high altitude. The air was thin, and the train moved much slower than it otherwise would have if it were travelling at sea-level. At times, the track would skirt the high cliff-edge, delicately balanced upon the sheer drop which descended for thousands of feet below. For a train that was named 'the Express' colloquially, it ran extremely slowly, even after it had got up to what was presumably its top speed.

The empty, arid landscape was only occasionally broken by lines of trees planted by the railway's flanks, which created dark shady tunnels of leaves - though the deeper they delved into the desert, the more sporadic these shelters became.

On the appearance of a small settlement growing out of the horizon, Roberto felt the great machine slow down slightly, its brake pads screeching out and echoing off into the distant setting sun. Going now at little more than a walking pace, the buildings approached, revealing an outpost, scantily supplied with a few soldiers and minimal infrastructure, so isolated that it made you wonder why any person would wish to inhabit such a barren neck of the woods. A few of the soldiers ran alongside the opened freight carriages, exchanging sacks of letters, provisions and other basic necessities. Judging by the size of the stuffed postbags, it had been a long time since the Express had passed through.

As quickly as it had arrived however, the outpost departed in the opposite direction from the train, which gradually picked up speed again after all the exchanges of goods had been completed. This process of loading and unloading, without the train ever stopping, was repeated a few times in similarly disparate stations along the route to the city.

Before long, the peak of the white Mino Tower of Ballyna poked up from beyond the horizon, shining gold in the soft evening sun. As it set slowly into the eastern sea, its fading orange embers brightened up this limestone column which arose from a checkerboard town of black basalt buildings and chalky white stone, both carved from the cliffs above the ocean. The Mino Tower stood tall on the highest point of the hill that the city was centred upon, which projected it even further beyond the light fog which sporadically covered the town.

Capt. Clint explained how the black mound at the base of the tower was an ancient volcano, where the Falconer's Black Temple was carved into the former crater. The Mino Tower had been built from within this temple, as part of a peace agreement made between the many communities who had moved into the surrounding hillside over the years.

Its construction was completed equally by the three main groups of peoples; namely, the Astrognomers, the Falconers, and the Folk, the last of whom looked much the same as you or I, alongside a coalition of smaller groups of domesticated animals. The Astrognomers however, being a weaker bunch considering their smaller stature, instead took on much of the designing and architectural work, rather than the heavy lifting of stone. This meant that the inside ceilings and rooms were designed for much lower heads than most, and made the apartments and offices mostly suited to the needs of the Astrognomers, thereby becoming almost solely inhabited by them.

As the city's lights grew nearer, joyful music arose from its walls, echoing throughout the empty desert the train was lumbering across. Pipes and tambourines and violins and accordions bounced off the flat stone buildings now lit with torches as the day grew into a darker shade of blue.

113

Off in the approaching distance, two wooden gates covering the path of the track into the city's walls were pulled back to allow the Express' passage within. Its carriages squeezed through the gap and passed, snake-like, along the town's spiralled main street, winding up towards the Black Temple and Mino Tower.

The entire train was being brought inside the walls, so as to be able to be unloaded overnight. The foremost dozen or so carriages reached the station's platform which lay on the opposite side of a central square, Place Agavé, which housed the grand sculpted entrance to the monotone monolith. A steep straight street led sharply down to the harbour, cutting back on itself occasionally, when the hillside became too steep. To the west there was a flatter street, lined with restaurants filled with all sorts of everyones, all different types of peoples, sat at outdoor tables, merrily enjoying their evening meal.

Roberto & Geronimo got down onto the black pavestones, and followed the group across the square towards a group of twelve people. Four Astrognomers, four Falconers, and four Folk. The Twelve remained silent, observing Roberto & Geronimo for a while from a distance, before stepping back towards the entrance and conversing together in hushed hurried tones.

Whispering orders into a guard's ear, their dark robes disappeared once more within the sombre shadows of the temple. The Elders had deemed the findings 'worthy of further investigation' and had Roberto & Geronimo escorted to the uppermost floor of the tower, to await the outcome of the Process.

A large pallet passed by them, entering the temple's central hall, carrying upon it the rusted throne, alongside a plaster replica of the fountain's statues. The pair moved through the crowded entranceway into the dimly lit cavern, just about able to make out many black and white etchings on the walls. The Two Sisters, Hélène & Belén, were watching over the comings and goings of all the clerical workers inside, shuffling papers and exchanging materials for payments of gold and silver coins.

Hélène was always drawn in a black, veiled dress, slightly taller than the white-gowned Belén, who seemed the more joyful of the pair. No-one apart from Roberto appeared to take much notice of these carvings, likely having seen them many times prior, instead focusing on the busy trading floor below. Santos & Clint took leave of them now, excusing themselves to take part in a series of briefings and de-briefings detailing their discoveries. A stout Astrognomer took over as the chief 'companion' to the 'guests' and brought them to the grey marble staircase which led upstairs to the bright Mino Tower. Up and on they climbed, past identical offices filled with grumpy workers, some of whom lazily looked towards the passing company, saluting them as they went.

At length (or height) they reached the observatory on top, where many Astrognomists were busy studying the skies above. A small apartment had been set aside for the 'guests', where they entered and had the wooden door shut behind them by their 'companion.' When they asked his name, he had told them it was simply easier if they just called him 'Friend.'

The room was sparse. White sheets on white furniture built from pale silvery wood. A gold telescope stood beside the window, angled upwards towards the skies. For a week, this room was their home, never leaving it bar Roberto's daily bathroom break, where he managed to spy the Astrognomers hard at work during his walk along the corridor leading to the bathroom. For the first days, the pair got along well, keeping each other amused in spite of having little else they *could* do.

But, after about the fourth day, they began to quibble and squabble over meaningless things, such as who had to set the table, (food being delivered at three regular mealtimes, though cutlery was not provided) or whose turn it was to bring out the garbage. Every evening however, after they

115

had eaten their dinner, they would gather round the telescope to look at the night sky.

They were amazed to discover the variety of colours which lit up the dark dusky sky. From the ground (or with their own eyes at least), the stars seemed to be a mostly uniform shade of white, but with the telescope's magnification, they could see a multitude of reds, blues, oranges, greens, and yellows emanating from distant galaxies.

One evening however, Capt. Clint came to visit them after supper. He was able to show them the other half of the sky, the empty darkness. This was the key difference in how the Astrognomers and the Falconers perceived the world. Where the Astrognomers admired the stars, the diamonds, the fleeting flowers around them, the Falconers focused instead on the green stalks the flowers bloomed upon, the earth which covered the diamonds, and, most importantly, the darker portions of the night sky. What seemed barren of beauty to the Astrognomers' eyes was where the Falconers pointed their telescopes, delving into the open oceans of black to search for that one fleeting supernova, exploding so far off that there was no way of quantifying how long it would take for people like them to reach it.

In this way, he showed them a secondary dance of celestial movements, which had always been there, yet they had been without the patience and awareness to see it previously. With an unobstructed view upwards, (for, you will remember, they were above most of the clouds, up there in the tower) their entertainment during their captivity mostly consisted of looking up at night, and then down at the town during the day.

This too, it seemed, occupied the Astrognomers throughout the day, though Roberto didn't approve of the workers following suspicious-looking people through the streets - suspicious, that is, to the Astrognomers' eyes. Ostensibly, (whatever that means) the observers argued that their job was to aid the police of Ballyna to arrest criminals, though there was so little crime in the city that there was almost no reason for this level of surveillance. At the very least, the telescope allowed Roberto & Geronimo to learn a little bit about the life of the cityzens from afar.

Their window looked out over the sea, which took up most of the view, but way down below, out where the land met the blue waters, they saw the largest ship you could imagine. A great big galleon, kilometres long, a good few across too, resting within the circular harbour. Even with the telescope, it was difficult to follow all the goings-on going on aboard the moored behemoth. Legions of people were busy hoisting boards and hammering nails to add yet another storey to the uppermost deck, though the titanic beast *did* appear to be approaching completion.

It bore its name – 'La Providencia' – on its port bow, silver letters on golden-brown wood, alongside small canoes and boats which dangled haphazardly astride the hull, all strung up with knotted hemp ropes. Almost all of these were white, with black accents drawn across their edges, though several had splashes of red and blue to distinguish themselves. At first glance, they seemed rather uniform, though upon further inspection, Roberto could see that each of the small windows surrounding the open cabins were all unique, some had large round potholes, others had wide angular screens, and others were, quite frankly, rather plain.

The height of the Tower made it difficult to look down at the town itself, but where they could see out, down on the port, there were many small fish markets, where old men with peak caps dried and salted their daily hauls. Their equipment was simple, yet highly efficient.

Every morning, Roberto & Geronimo would crowd around to watch the fishermen march through the deserted marketplace to the wharf, and take up their butterfly-shaped nets before battling the approaching white tide. Struggling out through the broken surf, they waded up to their knees, before getting into their vessels.

Sticking out from each side, the wide stiff nets looked like two wings, allowing the fishermen to draw up their nets and sieve away any small fry, to leave only the largest, meatiest fish. Then, once they had their fill, they came back in to land, just before lunchtime, arriving on the shore like a flock of migrating swallows. This cycle repeated itself each weekday without fail.

Just as consistent as this were the stars each night, radiating across eons to meet their eyes. Geronimo was convinced that he had watched one go out, though Roberto was sure he had seen another appear nearby. After a week of isolation, a triumphant knock came upon the door, brap-a-brap-brapbrap!

At a moment's notice, the door swung back to reveal a small committee, comprising the same consortium they had travelled with, with General Santos at its forefront. Removing from his pocket a small scroll of parchment, he stood up straight and announced:

'I can hereby, herewith, herewithout, with you here, and I there, declare that in accordance with Section B of the rules laid out during the First Process, that you, Roberto & Geronimo, have successfully passed The Trial!'

The pair looked at each other in confusion ('Wasn't it called The Process beforehand?' they thought) as a cheer went up from the gathered crowd. It was unclear what exactly this would mean for them, before Capt. Clint, dutybound as ever, took them aside and explained in layman's terms that 'You will join us on our expedition. You've surely seen the Providencia moored in the harbour? Well, its two-hundred-year construction is nearing a close, and it will finally be set sail towards The Horizon.'

With this decree, the pair were ushered out of the room and across to the high-roofed domed observatory at the top of the tower. It was evening now, so the white walls and diamond chandeliers glowed gold, leaving a fiery tone in the air. A ceremonial procession followed within the observatory, anointings and appointments with makeup artists, bows and gestures that seemed awfully formal, before the pair were marched through the crowd and down the tower. The Black Temple's central hall was quieter than before, sombre too, in the oncoming dusk.

Out into the street and down the hill towards the harbour, where tall yellow cranes stood guard against the soft setting sky. Windy breezes whipped across the wide flat boulevards that stretched from the bottom of the hill towards the port. Arched arcades housed many small grocer's shops, each square block being a single interconnected marble building, most with steeple and clocktowers, all made in miniature of the Mino Tower's architecture.

White restaurants packed with customers watched the parade of people being brought down towards the grand Providencia's shadow, a real castle on the water, astonishingly large when you got close to it. Great galleons parked alongside were dwarfed by this gargantuan mass of activity on the mammoth's decks.

Shops and houses adorned the thriving community onboard it, filled with various cultures ready to set off together to find The Horizon. United under one spiralled symbol emblazoned upon each and every ship of the fleet they awaited the swiftly approaching departure. From the dark shadow of the ship, the great white pillar on the hill seemed even larger now, shining out in the evening sun.

La Providencia would, after decades in construction, commence its natal naval voyage into The Horizon at the beginning of the next day, which for the people of Ballyna, was the hour that the moon rose.

VIII
Providencia

The sun had set around half-way to eight, (which is what *they* called half-past seven) leaving the twilight-tinted heavens above empty, except for the stars and constellations. It was during this time that the sailors adjusted their maps and compasses, calibrating their equipment in accordance with that night's sky.

Then, at around eleven o'clock, the moon emerged from the forest beyond the distant Zapateca mountains, covering the great empty desert with a silvery glow, slivering over Ballyna, up the great white tower and down towards the harbour where a glass was broken upon the ship's hull as the Providencia departed. Slowly. It took a long time for that great hulk of wood and metal to be pushed even a metre away from the land of San Salvador.

Roberto & Geronimo had been shuffled onto the ship during those few hours between days (for the sunset ended the day which had started at the previous moonrise) and were delivered once again to quite a comfortable residence in the ship's stern, only this time they were given the keys to the door, and subsequently, free roam of the ship.

Dinner was no longer provided to their rooms however, and they were each given a satchel of 'Providencia Pounds' which they could exchange in any one of the fine dining establishments located along La Gallerie, where there was a restaurant to meet just about every budget. The uppermost deck was lined with streets of shops and restaurants, squares and parks and all the other trappings you would expect to find in the city centre of any small European tourist destination.

Walking along beneath the swaying palm trees and streetlights, Geronimo began to feel somewhat nauseous, so they stopped into a café to drink some water and allow Geronimo to rest in a cosy corner compartment.

'Why, welcome to the party!' said a smooth silky voice from the table behind. Captain Clint was out drinking with five of his closest friends in the next booth over. The Falconers were now dressed in lighter evening gear, brown robes without a hood, revealing their heads, which had previously been covered.

'I didn't recognise you in those clothes!' said Roberto, Geronimo queasily poking his head around to greet the company, before sliding back down into the corner.

'We only wear them during the daytime,' said the man at the Captain's right-hand side.

'…and at celebrations,' added another.

'This ship has been twenty-three decades in the making,' said the Captain, 'and we were much older when it began construction. Growing up in its shadow, which would grow larger month by month, it's a pleasure to finally see it set free.' There was a hint of pride in these final words.

'That's all well and good,' chirped in Geronimo, now getting back to his usual, upbeat self, 'but how exactly are we supposed to sail ONTO the Horizon?'

'We must watch the moon,' said the older, quieter man to the left of the Captain. 'It will pass through its faces, and look different each night for almost a moonth (or a February, to be exact), before becoming full once again. That is the moment. When that happens, we must light the rockets, and take aim for the liquid shores at the Horizon's edge.'

'Sounds like a pretty silly thing to me – how do you know it will work?' Geronimo cheekily remarked.

'We hope it will,' came the rapid response.

Even though this seemed like a highly wishful basis upon which to sail off into open ocean with little more than a six-week supply of food and water, Geronimo had no real reason to doubt that which the Falconers had said.

'And what will we do if it doesn't work?' Geronimo persisted.

'It will. Have faith.' was the response, and the group's communal conviction permeated the air with such intensity that the pair did not need to ask again.

The moon was approaching the sky's zenith, making the streets too hot to navigate, so they remained there a couple of hours more, to avoid the glare of midday. After a good few hours of merrymaking with Capt. Clint and his band of Falconers, the moon had passed just beyond the main mizzenmast, creating shade on the boat's top deck. Geronimo was feeling better now, his first, but not his last, bout of seasickness now left behind him.

The Providencia too was now leaving the harbour, at half a snail's pace and out onto the wide glassy ocean. Barely a breeze was blowing that night, the small pilot engines were quietly guiding and tugging the great lumbering turtle out of the bay, yet a party-like atmosphere lingered in the rearmost quarters. The admiral and captain's cabins were both located back here, General Santos' room above Capt. Clint's one, both bedecked with golds and jewels heaped upon silver doors.

Santos, or Admiral Santos as he preferred to be called when out in open ocean, was rarely seen outside his room throughout the first few days, holding many secret covenants and late-night meetings with a select group of his closest aides. Clint, however, was often seen in the bars and streets of La Providencia, keeping the peace atop his camel Cheyenne, upon whom he rode side-saddle.

It was through these chance meetings that Geronimo & Roberto would learn about the vast aquatic world which surrounded them. There were clusters of small, crescent-winged birds called 'swifts' that dotted hither and thither above the surface, looking for fish to eat.

'Those wee blighters never stop moving you know; they spend ten out of twelve months of the year in flight. Everything they do in their lives is done without breaking a stride – you see how they go up high and then glide back down like a kite? They're drawing out paths for the others to follow.'

The Captain became much more animated than usual when he was discussing avian matters, and clearly had much more information he wished to tell, though he could always sense the right moment to leave a conversation, leaving it to linger longer in the listener's memory.

When riding Cheyenne, Clint would don a small pair of round goggles to protect his eyes from the wind. His gaze seemed magnified behind these, microscopically admiring each new bird he would see. Of course, he would always have his Falcon close at hand, resting upon his shoulder, sweeping off at will to inspect a new pocket of marine life.

Days passed. Weeks passed. Soon, they had nearly spent twenty-three days onboard the ship. The land was slowly drifting away behind them, the moon was blossoming, becoming ripe, and now beginning to wane. In just a few days, it would cloud over completely, leaving two nights barren of moonlight, before, as the Falconers predicted, once again rising triumphantly through the ocean, where they could greet it as she awoke.

Time passed differently out on the ocean. There were no clocks, no train timetables or opening times, days were sleepy and windy, nights were lively and gentle. Food was actually being grown onboard, in greenhouses above the engine room, way down in the great depths of the ship. She looked even mightier now, away from the land, sails unfurled, winds at their backs, heaving the behemoth off towards the marbled edge of the sky.

Four ballast masts with plump sails of cushioned air towered above the many streets beside La Gallerie on the toppermost deck. The shop signs all had little windmills perpendicular to the forward-facing gusts which tumbled down from the sails, storing energy in small batteries hooked up with some dodgy-looking wiring. Solar panels too, caught light like this, and by night would be used to power so many little bulbs that it was necessary to go out into the park to see the stars.

This, they did quite regularly, normally in Peregrin Park, at the mizzen-end of La Providencia, where many groups of Falconers would quietly convene around two o'clock each morning. There was one covert, but convenient bench located just off the main path, behind a row of deep pine trees, where Geronimo & Roberto would meet each night, for by now they had found many new activities that took each of their fancies during the evening. Yet, they would always keep their stargazing appointments, in rain or in moonshine.

'You know, I think the stars are shifting westwards, there's a new constellation over there in the East,' said Roberto one night, after their eyes had adjusted to the dim evening light.

'Yes, but the southern dog is slipping away below the Horizon!' cried Geronimo sadly. 'That one was my favourite, the sky was darker there, and it made those few stars shine even brighter.'

'Won't be long now until it slips over the Horizon,' replied Roberto, 'Where do you think it goes?'

'Well, if they follow the same trajectory as the moon, they most likely fall into the ocean like great big flaky snowballs – but how they come back out the other side is a mystery to me,' came Geronimo's studious response.

'Someone has been hanging out in the library I see!' jeered Roberto, who had been spending far too much of his own time just wandering around the ship, exploring its dimly-lit depths and chatting with all the strange folk he found there. 'I wonder what will happen over there, above the Horizon,' Roberto pondered aloud.

'Whatever will happen will happen,' stated Geronimo knowingly, who had grown rather wise, and rather plump, throughout their time on La Providencia.

'It won't be long either till the two dark days,' said Roberto, and it wasn't. As ever, the pair met up like clockwork at the same spot, at the same time on the first of these dark evenings, though they both had need of small lanterns to guide their paths. Once they were settled, observation apparatuses equipped, and eyes set starward, Roberto turned to Geronimo, saying, 'Don't they all seem a lot closer tonight?'

'Brighter too,' replied Geronimo, 'It's all to do with the curvature of the earth.'

This did not seem quite right to Roberto, but Geronimo had said it with such confidence that he could find little reason to doubt him. It did seem true though, to an extent. Up above, the black heavens seemed at once within reach, yet still a thousand miles off, spiky silhouettes of light illuminated against a stark background.

They were not alone out here either, as the days grew shorter, more and more Astrognomers and Falconers came out to the park, some of whom were even able to show Roberto & Geronimo a selection of 'dancers' – a rare phenomenon whereby several stars would wiggle and shoot off in the direction of the Horizon. These were a good sign; it meant that they were drawing close to the 'singyularatee' – the point where sky and sea meet.

Late on the second day, a heavy cloud grew on the Horizon. Thick and grey and bringing with it a sprinkling of stardust - small cold flakes which tickled your nose as they fell softly. As the second morning passed into the third day, time stopped making sense, and a bright white light began to glow

in the distance, bubbling on the water's edge. A faint rumble emanated from
it, like how you can feel a tractor shake the summer air before you can see it.

All the people on board would now begin their preparations for
departure, attendants waiting, soldiers at arms, rocket boosters ready to be lit.
A great arrangement of flowers and fruits was being built up upon the bow of
the ship, at the front of the foremast. General Santos (Admiral Santos at sea,
he didn't forget to remind them!) emerged from his cabin for the first time in
almost a week, having been locked up in isolation to make ready his
ceremonial gown.

'The time is come! The stars draw hither!' He shouted from his
white linen shroud, stood like a shaman within a circle of gifts and offerings.
He withdrew another of those strange sticks of incense, lit it, and threw it at
his feet. The smoke whipped up violently in a gust of wind, Santos again
made those strange, grunting 'Broo-hah!' noises, and a hundred-fold flock of
seagulls whooshed overhead towards the bubbling light, which was now
approaching a starchy boil. The birds swarmed forward, ducking and diving as
one giant unit before plunging gracefully into the growing white foam.

Fish of all shapes and sizes were jumping up to slap their sharp fins
at the seagulls' snapping beaks. By the time the Falconer eye-glass watchers
had managed to report this fact in the Astrognomer tongue to the General
('Admiral at Sea!' he shouts), it was too late. Admiral Santos had already
loudly decreed for his men to 'Cut the cable! Drop the torches!' and in so
doing, had lit the rockets.

What you must remember, dear reader, is that all of this takes time
to write down, (and to read) but on the ship, everything was now happening
so quickly that you barely had time to see it.

La Providencia was now moving faster, slowly heaving its great bulk
forward thanks to the smoking thrusters at its rear, and this led to a sensation
in your stomach much like how a plane taking off from a runway pulls all your

insides backwards. The thriving mass of seagulls and fishes had now grown to such a frenzy that it was not exactly clear what was bigger, it, or La Providencia.

Naval officers and sailors shouted up from the decks, 'We're goin to hit her, Captain!' Admiral Santos was deep within his trance, 'Broo-ha, Bruhahhh!' and so, the charge of the ship was left to the command of Captain Clint Lewis Caribou.

He jumped astride his trusty camel Cheyenne, and rode her to the ornate shipfront to view the approaching bulky mass, through his circular spectacles. To his shipmates he shouted, 'It's too late to change course! We can only hope that she's gentle to us all!'

This 'she' was none other than Santos' beloved, the Bruja Belén, Mother of Moon & Ocean. She breached through the boiling foams in the shape of a great white whale, twice the length of La Providencia, with dark black eyes the size of castles. Slowly, she showed her arched, scaled back, glowing as silver as the moon on a particularly clear night. Slapping her tail upon the water she created a powerful wave, then she turned to swim off towards the clouds.

The ship was pushed backwards by both this and the tsunami of cold sands falling from those grey skies, but nevertheless it pushed through, wet and cold in the thickening storm. Several auxiliary ships with similar swirled designs upon their sails were being left behind in the chaos, too weak to withstand the barrage of sand and salty water, their smaller statures unable to hold themselves together as tightly as La Providencia.

Just as it seemed like they were approaching the whale, it would violently whip up another series of waves to repel her followers. At length, the Providencia came close, drawing alongside the gargantuan beast, which began to buffet and pummel the ship's sides with its brutal head. Splinters flew and cannons fired, and when Roberto & Geronimo looked around, they could barely see each other through the din, weighed down with pieces of broken wood, sandy flakes, and salty spray. The sky was bright and dark at the same time, much like a summer's twilight that is being covered over by an approaching layer of oncoming overnight rain.

'Our fuel is nearly out, Captain!' shouted the boys at the back.

'One last push, fellas!' came the guidance from Clint.

Santos' ritual was approaching a feverish pitch, his eyes were rolled back in their sockets, and he was sweating profusely. 'Brūhāna-nē-nī-nō' he cried, amongst other gibberish. The crew paid so little attention to him now that he probably wouldn't even have noticed if they had referred to him as General.

Schools of dolphins encircled the Providencia, routing it from behind and on its starboard flank, corralling it in on the opposite side of Belén, swimming parallel to the ship's port side. Since she was now so close, a few scraggly trees could be seen growing on her back, snapping like coral as she slammed her weight against the smooth sides of the ship, which was holding up remarkably well against the onslaught of forces it came up against.

Though, that's not to say that the big ship itself stood as solid as a rock under the immense pressure of the waves pushing against its front, and the fireworks display shooting out from behind. Rocking back and forth to the pulsating knocks from both left and right, Geronimo began to feel queasy once again.

'Oh Roberto, I haven't felt this ill since that first departure night.'

Roberto could see it in Geronimo's rounded face that he was not in a good way. Roberto had been feeling quite useless throughout this whole ordeal. Every person onboard seemed to be put to good use by some task or another, yet he and Geronimo were just left to their own devices (namely the telescopes and other measuring apparatuses).

'This is my moment to shine.' He thought, and grabbed a nearby cart to hoist his friend upon. It was easier said (written) than done however. Geronimo presently weighed around two-hundred Providencia Pounds – the aretē blob now making up most of this weight, though his green head had also hardened up substantially, gaining more of an oak-y texture, colour and weight.

They passed many valiant men shoring up the disintegrating ship, being blasted repeatedly by the aquatic army that surrounded them. Harpooners were plucking their instruments to a lilting tune - the harps' strings being designed with such a sleek material that their rich tones could soothe some of the dolphins to sleep.

When at last they arrived at the hospital tents, aided by a few friendly knights of the helm, the hospitaliers were far too occupied to receive them, their beds all already filled with brave young soldiers, bloody and splintered by the debris which flew through the smoggy air.

'With any luck, you might find a free ward up in the midship, reports tell us that there are far fewer casualties up there,' a young nurse told them, and whom they obliged to return to his duties swiftly, taking up as little of his time as possible, but not forgetting to thank him sincerely before trudging the cart further onward. One of the knights, a Falconer, sent his bird off ahead, to forewarn the doctors at the middle of the ship of their imminent arrival.

Once they got there, a white clinical tray was brought forward to transfer Geronimo into the 'Health Hub' – a pleasant enough name for a grim greystone block of nursing wards and medical units. It was built around the ship's main-mast, which grew up like a great grey tree trunk from its centre. Antennae and aerials sprouted from the pinnacle, flashing red and green many kilometres up in the air. Its walls were plastered with that strange falling dust – thinner than snow, yet coarser than sand.

Geronimo was rushed off inside, taking a deep look at Roberto as they were separated by a group of inspecting doctors. Roberto tried his hardest to get inside too, but deep down he knew he would only be getting in the way. Instead, he asked one of the knights who had helped him, how he could be of assistance.

'You could man the radios for us, up at the top there,' pointing up to the towering mast, 'I'm not sure what time it is exactly - if it's time for the AMFM or the PMFM – but just take a look at the heavens and play whatever you feel is appropriate for that moment in time.'

This was just the task for Roberto, who had quite a good taste for radio-friendly hits, particularly Motown and Stax records from their heyday in the 1960s. He scurried off towards the tower, nodding to the Falconers as he went. Most of the climb was easy enough, spiralled staircases swirling upwards, narrowing as they went higher and higher to the very top, where a control panel was set before a panoramic window.

The full size of Belén was now obvious, her blowhole was as big as the craters on the moon, with a bulky forehead built for headbutts, the lumpy masses bulging from all over its front. Strangely, there was little noise to be heard up here.

Down on the deck, hundreds of colliding noises merged to create an (almost) soothing white noise, but away on this exposed outpost, the wild winds seemed to blend into the stars' silence. Roberto scoured the first box of discs he could find, quickly settling on 'Respect' performed by Otis Redding, removing its sleeve, placing it on the turntable (ask your parents what that is), and then turning on the power.

A great spark flew out and thumped (with a few thuds) a booming, bellowing blow, and Roberto had just enough time to see everything around him morph into a green, mossy, earthy material. It all happened in about six seconds. Vines whipped out from the hospital below where he had last seen

Geronimo. These vines stretched their liquid-y brown arms all the way to the ends of the ship just as fast a lightning bolt. Then, a blinding white flash came from the sky as they snapped towards the whale, its silvered glow permeating through the bronze goo which kept expanding and was now merging into the pieces of stone-like snow falling through the air.

Capt. Clint & Cheyenne watched, helplessly, as this loamy metallic liquid filled the decks of the Providencia, drowning men and weighing down the bows towards the ocean's roar. Stooping down to test it, Clint noticed it was of the same consistency as the 'aretē' that Geronimo was so fond of. It was soothing to touch, and in those few seconds that remained before he was engorged by its flow, he looked upwards at the electrified mast, shockingly white, despite the aretē's best efforts to the contrary... before the base cracked, and it all came slowly tumbling down.

Amongst these great slabs of concrete and timber, like soft summer rain, Roberto was once again, falling.

IX
Samsara

Everything was white. Everything was still.

Feeling crept into Roberto's face.

Whatever he was laying on was cold, almost damp, and hard as rock.

Clean, pure air pushed into his nostrils.

A distant, but growing ringing noise filled his ears.

It came closer, and closer, before it slapped his face from right to left, and he rolled onto his back, awake, but still blind.

All of his sensations were coming back to him, his fingertips touched each other, he began to feel his legs, yet all he could see was a single shade of white, so white, that he couldn't even see his hands' shadows move in front of his face.

He sat up, and tried to stand.

It certainly felt like he was standing, but without actually seeing his own body, he was finding it hard to believe himself.

'Mountains of clouds, skies of seas, isles of stars, rains of rocks, mountains of clouds, skies of seas…' said a gentle voice, both close at hand and distant. It repeated these twelve words over and over, echoing around itself till the phrases had blended themselves together like a verbal waterfall, resonating not only through Roberto's head, but within his very being.

As these words came and went, passing over him like a rushing stream of cool mountain water, visions of clouds and oceans and islands and stones grew within his mind's eye, though even his thoughts appeared colourless – thick black lines sketching the shapes, shuffling around like string, as they painted the next image's wiry frame.

This sort of scene would normally make you feel quite nauseous, though after a month at sea, Roberto had begun to grow a strong pair of sea legs.

> 'Welcome' said the same voice as before, though this time it echoed from directly in front of Roberto.
>
> 'Who are you?' he asked cautiously.
>
> 'I am everything.' It boomed gently, a difficult sound to describe, the sort of soft voice that makes your heart flutter.
>
> 'If you are everything, then why can't I see you?' he asked, without really thinking his question over before he had said it.
>
> 'Well, since I am everything, that also means I am nothing. Everything is a very big thing, that's why we don't really have a word for it.'

Roberto thought about this for a moment.

The voice made a very good point.

'Does this mean that you are everywhere?'

'It means I am everywhere AND nowhere, at the same time.'

This idea had Roberto stumped for what felt like a long time, perhaps a minute, perhaps a second, perhaps a day.

There was no real way of knowing within that void.

The only thing that he could use to keep track of anything at all was the size of his own thoughts.

'If you are both everywhere, and nowhere, surely that must mean that you are somewhere?'

'Very well said, my child.'

The voice seemed closer now.

'Take my hand.'

This was easier said than done.

Roberto raised his right hand, and reached forward.

Nothing doing.

He stretched it out, out as far as he could, then suddenly, an icy spark of fiery pain shot up from his palm, up his arm, and into his chest.

His lungs felt like they were exploding, his head expanding, but as quickly as it had begun, it was over, and a tall woman stood before him. She was easily about eight-foot tall (or three metres, for all our American readers).

Her hair hung in long, brown ringlets all down her slender neck, falling all the way down to the bottom of her back, and she adjusted it gently, tucking it softly behind her left ear with her one free hand.

Her face was indescribably beautiful, in a way, she resembled Hana, who Roberto never could quite forget, only much older, with a womanly sort of wisdom that only comes with age and experience.

She glided softly forwards, taking long strides across the pale, silky sands that lay below her bare feet.

The loose white dress she was wearing trailed behind, covering their tracks, and leaving no trace of where they had been walking.

The ground was as smooth and flat as this in every direction, stretching off into what I suppose you could call a Horizon, but really, it was just the point where your eyes could see no further, and where the ground that they stood on joined up with the infinite black sky above.

On and on they walked, until Roberto finally picked up the nerve to ask,

'Where are we going?'

'Somewhere.'

Though this was certainly true, the answer did not exactly satisfy Roberto's curiosity.

After another long silence, he asked shyly, 'Do you have a name?' – realising that his previous attempt to obtain this information was imprecise.

The answer he had received before was indeed the right one for the question he had asked – 'Who are you?' - but was not the answer he had hoped to hear.

'I have had many names, but you can call me Hélène.'

Upon her face was a stony, proud expression, as grand as a statue on a plinth.

'This place is the space between spaces,' she continued, answering Roberto's question the very moment it began to grow in his mind. 'Above us, is darkness, below us is light. But here is where I reside, out of day, and out of night.'

Roberto followed her as she walked. He was slightly slower, since he struggled to keep up with her long, commanding strides.

Her thick thighs rippled her white dress, creating dark creases which trickled down onto the ground.

Her face however, had a more subtle, off-white colouration to it, her features sketched in a soft grey tone, like a pencil on a smooth sheet of paper.

This place had a strange aura about it. You could clearly see that nothing was around you for miles, yet it always felt like there was a rustling somewhere behind you - the sort of soft sounds that birds make when they scratch through twigs on a breezy afternoon, or waves crashing against a shore, only on the other side of a hill.

Then there was the sound that his feet made as they padded across the loose ground, crunching gently like fresh snows – as refreshing as, but not as cold as snow - about as temperate as the sea feels on a hot, sweaty day.

Eventually, after an indefinite amount of time walking straight ahead in a straight line, a glimmer appeared on the Horizon.

As they got closer to it, Roberto could clearly see that it was a throne, built of shabby brown wood with rusted metal edges, which, he thought, might have once been the same colour as the silver ground that they walked on.

It was rather plain for a throne, no ornate carvings or plump cushioned armrests, instead it was adorned with straight sharp lines and functional edges.

Roberto realised that this must be the throne of Hélène, and thought it would be polite if he were to kneel before her, as she bowed down her head before it.

From the corner of her eye, she spotted this, before lifting her strong head backwards to let out a loud, hearty laugh that seemed to shake the very air around them.

'What are you kneeling for?!' she exclaimed.

'I thought it would be respectful.'

'You should never kneel before anyone – especially not those who tell you to do it.'

Roberto returned to his feet, blushing shyly as he nodded towards The Lady.

'You can sit on it if you'd like,' as she beckoned him to come forward.

'After all, it's just a chair, and you've come a long way.'

Roberto felt it rude to decline her invitation, stepping meekly up and sitting on its edge.

'Go on, sit up straight Roberto, rest your back against it – Yes, that's it.'

Something about that chair made you feel like a king - but not a pompous one – a generous one who pays back out all the taxes he receives on things like roads and farming subsidies, not on pointless things like his own army or tax collectors.

Here Roberto sat, looking out at the vast swathes of black and white which unfolded before him, and at Hélène, the only thing there that broke up that line where the two colours met.

She gazed up lovingly at him, with enough emotion in her eyes to fill both cheering crowds and weeping congregations.

A single amber tear grew in her eye, a waxy bronze drop, and fell onto the back of her hand, where a golden harp appeared as it fell.

Her hands flowed over it, playing a deeply melancholic melody, that burned your heart to hear.

She sang a wistful lullaby in a tongue that sounded older and more ancient than time itself.

> 'Why are you crying?' Roberto asked her, noticing at the same time how the white ground appeared to be showing a hint of green, and the black dome above was softening into a dark navy morning light.
>
> 'I cry with joy, because I am the beginning of all things, and I cry with sorrow, for I must also be the death of all things.'
>
> 'B..b…but where will I go to? What will I be?'
>
> 'Fear not, child, for I am everywhere, the sky, the sea, the ground beneath your feet.
> I have been, and always will be, everything you have done, or ever will do.

Why, I'm even there in the words you speak –
Your A's, your B's and your C's'

Visions of all that Roberto had seen on San Salvador came back to him, as
Hélène sang these words to the tune of her harp. Alfred & Albert, Bidon &
Byron, Clint & Cheyenne, and many, many more, several pairs forging great
teams together.

It wasn't clear whether it was he, or Hélène who was fading, but soon
Roberto found himself in a field of thick grass, beneath a pale blue sky.

As she disappeared from view, Hélène gazed deeply one last time into
Roberto's very soul, and spoke to his deepest fears and desires, saying;

'We all must go someday.
Where will you go to?
Your breath will become the wind,
Your hands will become one,
Your eyes will become stars,
Your words will become poems,
Your dreams will become books,
And You will become
A part of the Earth once more.'

So here I am. Alone. Again.

Afloat once more upon the Samsaric Ocean.

Nothing has finished. Nothing has begun.

The waves run backwards.

That is, if they run at all. I, certainly, do not run. I do not even walk.

It is questionable what exactly I do at all.

At some point, there was a blinding flash.

I do not know if I was its cause.

The whole ship disappeared.

Yet, strangely, it all became one. A hundred thousand souls perished that day. That is, if they ever existed at all. The transmigration of the soul. For some, that is the single most important tenet upon which their faith is built. If *that* is the case, then where did those hundred thousand souls go to?

Perhaps they became the new people that live here.

Perhaps they became the animals.

Perhaps they became the insects.

Perhaps they became the soil.

Perhaps they became the mushrooms.

Perhaps they became the plants.

Perhaps they became the air.

Perhaps they became the rivers.

Perhaps they became the mountains.

Perhaps they became the towns.

Perhaps they became the cities.

Perhaps they became the islands.

Aha.

Perhaps then, that is what I have become?

Yet still I float. Adrift. Unanchored. Abound. Unbound. *Wandering.*

Yes, that is it. Wandering.

Drifting from one point to the next. Though, I suppose, that *is* what islands do. Slowly.

Slowly, slowly, they drift from one shore to the next. Though don't we all do that?

Make a decision Geronimo! Make a decision Bokoro! Decide what you are! Is that even possible? How can I decide to be exactly what I already am? Surely I am them already? I am many.

Voilà! You are many! That is a start. Now. Who are the many? My inhabitants! Now. Hold it. You are talking to me. Yes. And if you are talking to me, that means *I* am separate from you. Does it? Surely it does! How else could you hold multiple truths at once? Who are you talking to then, if there is only you in there?

To Alfred. To Belén. To Clint.

To every damned soul that was cursed to meet that so-called 'good ship' La Providencia. Every last one of them ended where I began. All that they lived for, all that they died for, all of it ended where I began. Where there were many, now there are one. Or maybe, there really are none.

I still have not quite worked out what exactly I am. Nor where I belong. Nor where I begin. Nor where I end. All that death. All that destruction. The splintered bodies and the spilled blood. Where did they all go to? What did they become? *Who* is even left to remember them?

I do, at least. Maybe you do too? *Why* do you remember them? Were they worth remembering? So many questions and so few answers.

Back to the most important question. Who am I?

I am Geronimo. At least I know that. I am also something else.

A blank slate. An open ocean. *A white whale.*

More than any of that, I am alive!

I'm still not quite sure what happened on that ship - Roberto brought me to that hospital block, the nurses rushed me away, I had another bout of nausea, and then

BOOM! Everything changed. Everything ended. Everything began!

All at once, it all seemed so real. Anything that I had felt before, seemed so unnecessary. Suddenly I felt the ground. Suddenly I felt the sea. Suddenly I felt life!

At first, it felt like there were many insects crawling all over me. A thousand pitter-pattering little insects, tip-tapping over everything that I could feel. A tingling and then sensation.

Then, I felt the birds, picking at each of these insects, and the plants sprouting from the soil to protect the insects. Slowly but surely, life grew, yes, life grew wildly.

Foxes grew up to kill the birds and then farmers grew too to cull the foxes. Such is life.

Before I knew it, there were things crawling here and there all over my back!

Yet now, I'm beginning to feel the weight of it all.

I once was young. Perhaps I still am.

I am not old, though I am certainly not young anymore.

Where exactly that leaves me, what exactly that *makes* me, I do not know.

Around and around, I go again.

Nothing has ever really ended.
Nothing will ever truly begin.

Nothing has ever really begun.
Nothing will ever truly end.

FIN

Printed in Great Britain
by Amazon